3

AND THEY FOUND
DRAGONS
RISE OF THE LIGHT BRINGER

TED DEKKER & RACHELLE DEKKER

ISBN (Paperback Edition): 978-1-7378675-2-4

Also Available in the And They Found Dragons trilogy:

The Boy Who Fell from the Stars (Book One)
ISBN: 978-1-7378675-0-0 (Paperback Edition)

Journey to the Silver Towers (Book Two)
ISBN: 978-1-7378675-1-7 (Paperback Edition)

Published by:
Scripturo
350 E. Royal Lane, Suite 150
Irving, TX 75039

Cover art and design by Manuel Preitano

Printed in the United States of America

CHAPTER ONE

S AMMIE clearly remembered the events that had delivered her to the dragons' lair, but they felt more like a dream than reality. Maybe all of this was a dream. Maybe her coming to Earth on a shuttle with Jack and Marco and Miguel was just a figment of her imagination. Maybe Marco's and Miguel's deaths were only part of a nightmare—although, to be honest, she didn't seem to mind them dying as much as she thought she should.

A great Red had swept in on the high plateau and rescued her from Jack's mission to kill the queen. She had agreed with the mission at one point but now saw it as an absurdity. Why she had ever supported killing such a magnificent creature was a mystery to her. Especially because only the queen could give her life through its milk.

It really did feel like a dream, and yet here she was, deep in the pitch-dark lair where the Red had brought her. Not a dream. She wasn't sure whether she should be terrified or comforted, because she felt both at the same time. Fear and comfort seemed to be the same thing here, as they had at the Scaler village. She wondered how that could be.

The stone under her knees was cold and smooth. Her palms and forehead rested against the ground. She dared not look up at the beast towering over her. She could hear movement in what she guessed was a large chamber—soft clicks and squishing sounds, like the sound of someone walking through mud—but her eyes didn't work in the darkness, so she could only imagine what the lair looked like. And even that was hard.

The queen's warm breath smelled like rotten eggs as it caressed her skin, sending a shiver through Sammie's body. It was a horrible scent, but a part of her loved that stench, because it came from the queen.

The queen's voice rumbled through the cavern, sharp and cold like a scolding mother. "You will bring me the boy from the stars."

Sammie swallowed and tried to speak, but her words got lost in her throat. She knew the queen was speaking only to her mind rather than using vocal cords to make sound, because that's how dragons seemed to communicate. And when she said "boy from the stars," she meant Jack.

An image of Jack's face filled her mind. He would never come!

Hearing her thoughts, the queen continued. "You must find a way. Use your connection to him. Do whatever is necessary but bring him before me."

Jack is too smart to be fooled now, Sammie thought. She'd have to force him, attack him when he least expected it and drag him before the queen. It would be the only way.

"He must come of his own free will," the queen said.

But that was impossible! To be certain the queen understood, she managed to whisper her concern aloud.

"He won't come," Sammie said.

"He must," the queen replied. "It is your honor to ensure that he does. Obeying me will give you life."

Comfort washed over Sammie's shivering body with the queen's warm breath. It was the royal beast's gift to all who feared her.

"Bring him to me, daughter," the queen said.

Sammie took a deep breath and settled into the queen's loving embrace. She knew then that she would do anything for her queen, by whatever means necessary.

"Good girl," the queen said. "You will not fail me."

"I won't," Sammie replied.

In that simple surrender to fear itself, Sammie went from trembling on the cave floor to feeling important and special. She would bring Jack to the queen, and he would finally see the dragon's true glory and power.

He would submit to the terror and comfort. Making him do so was Sammie's only purpose now.

"Good girl," the queen said again. "Now I will open your eyes so you can see."

As if a veil had been torn from her eyes, Sammie could see in the darkness.

And what she saw was beautiful.

CHAPTER TWO

J ACK CLUNG tightly to the dragon's silver scales as it dipped low toward the forest. He'd spent the night at the Silver Towers with Zevonus and the other silver dragons, feasting, laughing, and honoring the life and love of their fallen brother Tichondrius. Celebrating death as a passage was unlike anything Jack had ever experienced. If you had no fear of death, then what was left to fear?

His mother had often told him there was no fear in love, but he only understood it as a reality when he was among the Silvers, who knew only love. Although they mourned the passing of their friend, they took no issue with it, nor thought of it as anything more than the departure of Tichondrius from one place to another. He would be missed, that's all, and only for a short time, because they would all see him again soon.

Each Silver he'd encountered displayed the same

genuine love, and with each passing hour Jack's confidence in the truth of Yeshua grew.

When he'd woken with the rising sun, Jack knew beyond a shadow of a doubt what his path would be. The dragon king had to die if Earth was to be cleansed from the toxin of fear that ruled it. Only a redeemed Scaler could kill the dragon king.

He would offer the love of Yeshua to a Scaler, hopefully Camila, the daughter of the Village Mother, and show her the path from darkness to light. Then they would kill the dragon king together. Surely this was what his mother had sent him to do without knowing the specifics herself. The original mission to kill the queens would have failed, because the king would only make more queens. All would have been lost.

But now he had found the truth, and he was the only one alive who could save humanity from the red dragons' toxin. The thought was a little thrilling.

"We're nearing your fallen spacecraft, young Jack," the Silver he rode said to his mind.

"Thank you, Zeke," Jack said over the wind that whipped past his face.

He'd seen Zeke watching him with wide eyes at the feast last night, but he'd only met and melded with the younger dragon this morning. Zevonus had described Zeke as a young, enthusiastic Silver who'd completed his training and was ready to escort Jack on his mission. Upon being announced, Zeke had hopped down from a high oval platform with such joy and excitement that he'd nearly tumbled over his own clawed feet when he landed.

Jack smiled as he thought about the way Zevonus had cautioned Zeke to tame his excitement so as not to hurt himself. Zeke had straightened his back, held his head high, and said "Aye, aye, Captain."

Jack had liked Zeke immediately. He imagined that if dragons had the same expressions as humans, Zevonus would have rolled his eyes at the comment. Instead, the elder Silver had ignored the youngblood and gathered Jack in with his loving eyes.

"The calling you have accepted will not be easy," the Silver said. "Your journey out of fear will test you, mind, body and soul. Zeke will accompany you until you must continue alone."

"Alone?" Jack asked, blinking at the thought of losing the support of the Silvers.

"Yes, alone. But know that we will always be near."

Zevonus retrieved a small pouch from his scales. It was odd to see such a massive creature holding such a tiny parcel.

"This is for you," Zevonus said.

Jack took the blue velvet pouch from his extended claw. A simple silver tie held it shut.

"It's a gift," Zevonus continued. "Go on, take a look."

Jack untied the pouch and emptied its contents into his palm. A simple silver ring on a chain plopped into his hand.

"When the times comes, it will quicken love," Zevonus said. "Wear it hidden. You will know when it is needed."

Jack wasn't sure what "quicken love" meant, but he trusted Zevonus's promise. He slipped the chain around his neck and tucked the ring beneath his jersey.

"Go with light, young Jack. Be love in the darkness. Trust in the still voice that guides us all. Though you will walk through the valley of death, fear no evil. Fear nothing." The large dragon dipped his head in respect. "You are a light-bringer."

Jack felt a prick of sadness. "Will I see you again?"

Zevonus raised his head and held Jack's gaze for a long moment. "When you see with the eyes of Yeshua, you will have no need to see me again," he said.

He hadn't answered Jack's question, but Jack was sure their journey together wasn't over.

With a final goodbye, Jack climbed onto Zeke's back, and together they'd taken to the sky, headed for their first stop—Jack's shuttle.

Now, swooping over vast forests, imagining what "testing" awaited him on his "journey out of fear," as Zevonus had called it, Jack's confidence waned.

"Do not worry, young Jack," Zeke said, pulling Jack from his thoughts. "There's nothing to fear."

So said all the Silvers. But they were the manifestation of perfect love, in which there was no fear. Jack was still trying to understand that love.

"I'll cheer you up," Zeke said. "It has been said by many that I am skilled beyond measure in the art of flying."

Jack chuckled, because it sounded like something only Zeke, of all the Silvers, would say.

"It is true!" Zeke said. "I'll show you. Hold on tight."

Jack squeezed his knees together and gripped Zeke tightly, excitement nipping at his mind as the young Silver aimed his head straight up and surged high into the clouds. His leathered wings beat in quick movements as Jack clung to him.

"Don't worry! If you fall off, I will catch you," Zeke said, piercing the clouds.

Without warning, the dragon twisted upside down. Terror exploded inside Jack's chest, but before he could cry out, Zeke entered a full loop. The force of the turn pressed Jack into the dragon's back, filling him with relief. He allowed himself to feel the thrill of flying upside down. On a dragon, no less!

He let out a whoop and Zeke laughed full-heartedly as Jack squeezed Zeke's neck tighter.

"Watch this!" Zeke cried. He entered into a full

barrel roll, robbing Jack of breath. But Jack didn't fall off, and once more the thrill of flying upside down made him whoop. This time he laughed with Zeke.

"You like it?" the dragon asked.

"Yes, but I think I might get sick," he said.

"Yes, yes, of course." Immediately, Zeke slowed and resumed their set course for the shuttle. "See?" he said. "I have mad skills."

Jack smiled at Zeke's choice of words, wondering where he'd learned the expression. He wondered what Zevonus would have thought about Zeke's antics.

"There it is!" Zeke proclaimed.

Jack saw the shuttle through the trees below them, and Zeke swooped down, extended his wings, and landed on the cliff close to the Thunderbird. Marcos had fallen off this cliff, pushed by Sammie. He wondered where Sammie was now. Had the Red taken her back to the queen? Was she still alive? Maybe she was with the Scalers.

He pushed the thoughts from his mind as Zeke lowered his neck so Jack could climb down. Jack's legs were a bit shaky when he stepped onto firm ground, and he used Zeke to balance himself.

"You're trembling, young Jack," Zeke said. "Not to worry, it's a common reaction to my amazing skills."

Jack looked up and caught the Silver's wink. He

smiled. "So amazing, Zeke. Thank you for showing me just how amazing."

"Any time. We could go again now if you like."

"I'm good."

"Yes. So am I," Zeke said. "All good."

Jack chuckled. "All good."

The Thunderbird sat among the trees where they'd left it. He hoped all the supplies he and Sammie had been carrying were still in the pack they'd left on the plateau. His plan called for the blood kit in that pack, so the plateau would be their next stop. First he wanted to see if any communication from the Sanctuary had come through. He still didn't know if they'd received the Morse code message he'd sent a few days earlier.

"Come on," Jack said. "This shouldn't take long."

"I'll keep watch," Zeke said, stopping next to the trees.

Jack nodded and headed into the spacecraft. There wasn't much left. The Scalers as well as he and Sammie had raided the ship. Jack hurried over to the radio and switched it on, expecting to hear only static.

Instead, a steady string of beeps filled the cockpit. It took only a moment for Jack to realize he was hearing Morse code. His heart lurched. The Sanctuary must have received his message and returned their own on a continuous loop!

He quickly grabbed the same piece of paper and pen he'd used to write his first message and sat down to decode the transmission. Fingers flying, he jotted down the dots and dashes, desperate to hear from his mother.

Translating the code from memory, the message began to take shape. His excitement turned to concern. Jack thought he must have deciphered something incorrectly. He couldn't be hearing what he thought the message was saying. He ran through the code three times, checking and rechecking the letters on the page. There was no error.

Scrubber system failure. We have oxygen reserves for only seven days. We are beginning reentry protocols. Team Gamma assumed dead. Imperative you kill both queens. It's up to you now, my son. You are our only hope. I love you.

Jack read it again, his mind numb. The Sanctuary was running out of oxygen, and without functioning scrubbers they couldn't make more. They were coming to Earth. He thought he still had twenty days. Twenty days to change the heart of a Scaler so they could kill the dragon king and make Earth safe for his mother to return.

But seven days? The air felt thin. He needed more time!

Jack stood and started to pace, trying to take deep breaths. He couldn't think straight through the panic swarming his mind. What if he couldn't do this? What if he failed and humanity was lost?

"Do not get lost in fear, young Jack." Zeke's voice reached his mind through the blinding madness. "Return to light."

Jack placed his hand against shuttle wall to steady himself.

"Though you walk through the valley of death, you will not be afraid."

Jack focused on Zeke's words. If he couldn't get past his own fear, humanity would be lost forever. Earlier, he'd felt a small thrill at being the means of humanity's survival, but now it sounded like a terrible idea.

With a few more deep breaths, Jack managed to calm the trembling in his fingers.

He checked the time stamps of the message loop and found the code had been broadcasting for eight hours. They were nearly halfway through the first of seven days. He needed to send a reply. He wanted to tell his mother everything, but that would be too much.

Think, Jack. Calm down and think.

He leaned his head against the comms panel and closed his eyes. A wave of pain swallowed him at the idea of never getting to talk to his mother again. Jack pushed the idea away, took a final deep breath, and began tapping out his response.

"Message received," he said slowly as he entered the corresponding code. "Plan in place. Nothing is what we thought. Don't come until you must. I will do all I can to make it safe. Mom . . ." Jack's fingers started to shake again. He swallowed the raw emotions threatening to tear him apart. "I'm doing what you taught me. I love you."

Jack sent the message on a continuous loop and stepped back. Seven days. There was no time to waste.

Even as he climbed out of the shuttle, the plan in his mind started to shift. He didn't have the time to win Camila's trust. But if not her, then who? He needed things to happen quickly. Like tonight! Hopefully, he could still find the pack with the blood kit and jerky.

Jack hurried to Zeke, his brain racing through the task awaiting him.

"Don't be discouraged, young Jack," Zeke said. "A heart can change quicker than you think."

Jack noticed Zeke was staring at some boulders near the ledge. At the base of the largest rock grew several small red flowers with pointed petals.

"These flowers grow scarcely this time of year," Zeke said. "We call them dragon sleep, because their leaves induce sleep for even a dragon."

"What do they do to a human?" Jack asked.

"A single leaf would surely render a human of your size unconscious for hours. I would not suggest eating them."

Jack wondered if such a potent plant might serve him later. He pulled a single flower with three leaves from the patch and carefully tucked it in his pocket.

Zeke was giving him a funny look.

"You never know what I might need," Jack said with a shrug.

The Silver hesitated for a moment. "You never know. Are you ready to find your supplies on the plateau?"

Jack nodded and Zeke lowered his head so Jack could climb back onto his neck. Within seconds they were airborne, and Jack reviewed his new plan with the Silver. Within half an hour they were settling down on the plateau where Tichondrius had been killed by Lukas and Sammie had been taken by the Red.

The pack was still there. With a sigh of relief, Jack scooped it up and scrambled back up Zeke's neck.

"Got it!"

"Hold on, young Jack."

Then they were off again, headed to a spot Zeke assured him was the perfect location from which to approach the Scaler village.

The rocky clearing in the trees looked tiny from the

air, but as the dragon came in for a landing, Jack saw it was at least fifty paces wide—large enough for Zeke to maneuver in while still offering plenty of protection.

"Here we are!" Zeke said as Jack slid to the ground. "Does it meet your satisfaction?"

There was a pile of large boulders with a natural cave of sorts at one end, a good place for a small camp. "Good enough." Jack said.

"Perfect. Then I must leave you now. Remember, walk due east and you will find the village."

"You're leaving already?"

"Yes, this close to the Scalers, I must remain hidden. It's time for you to continue your journey out of fear. But rest assured, now that we are bonded I will be listening closely. If I am able, I will come quickly."

"What do you mean, if you are able?"

"In some situations, my physical presence may not be the best, young Jack. Don't worry, you will succeed. I believe in you."

Jack thought about that for a moment. "Did Tichondrius succeed? He ended up dead and I might too."

"But of course Tichondrius succeeded. Love cannot fail. From a human perspective, the success of love is not always apparent at first." Zeke turned to take flight, then looked back. "You are courageous to face such a great challenge, young Jack."

"Yes, but remember, I will need you tomorrow like we talked about. My whole plan depends on you."

"Yes, yes, of course. I will be here if I am able. But sometimes plans change."

With those disconcerting final words, the young dragon beat his wings, hauled his large body into the air, and quickly vanished over the nearest ridge. Jack knew that in Zeke's way of thinking without fear, he meant to encourage, but Jack's worry deepened. He couldn't shake the feeling that the challenge both Zevonus and Zeke referred to would be greater than he imagined.

The hours ticked by slowly as Jack waited for night-fall, and he felt himself becoming impatient. There was nothing more he could do except try to quiet his mind.

The sun was setting when Jack started toward the Scaler village.

By the time he reached the outskirts, the sun was gone and the bright stars were out. He knew the Scalers didn't have night patrols, because they had no enemies but the Silvers, who never attacked. Waiting for the village to bed down for the night, he climbed a tree. He felt safer up high than on the ground. Also, he could see and hear more clearly.

And he did hear—cries of anguish and fear followed by singing and rejoicing as the comfort came during the nightly ceremony. The sounds raised the hairs on the back of his neck. Couldn't they see that they were being manipulated by fear? What kind of god would demand to be feared? Not a God of love, because there was no fear in love.

The night had turned cold by the time all the sounds from the village ceased. It was time to go.

Heart in his throat, Jack climbed down from the tree and snuck forward. He reached the outskirts of the village and peered around a thick tree trunk. The large firepit under the raised dragon skull still glowed with embers from the ceremony. Wind coming off the mountains ruffled the leaves and sent a shiver down Jack's spine. The village lay dormant, not a soul to be seen. Nothing stirred, no voices carried.

This was Jack's moment. Remaining in his crouched position, he started toward the village center. Quickly, careful not to make any sound, Jack passed a few huts as he angled for the glowing firepit.

His heart pounded in his ears and he tried to calm his breathing as he reached the ring of stones. He slid his pack off his back and dug out a note he'd written earlier.

Camila, meet me in the clearing two miles west. I have information about the

Silvers you will want to hear. Come alone.

Jack

He placed the note against one of the metal poles that held up the dragon skull and secured it with a piece of twine. He knew this was a risk, but he had to get Camila to meet with him.

The wind whipped again and the corners of the note rippled. Jack feared it would come loose, so he secured more twine to the top and bottom to hold it in place.

A stick snapped somewhere deep in the woods behind him and he froze. Time to get out of here, he thought.

He knew it was a long shot. Camila would probably not come to him alone. But if anyone would come, it would be her. She had nothing to fear from him, a small boy with a fraction of her strength.

Jack turned and hurried for the cover of forest. All he could do now was get back to the clearing and wait.

CHAPTER THREE

SIX DAYS, Michelle thought, holding the transcript in her trembling hands. It isn't enough time!

She lifted her head and stared at her reflection in the mirror. Her eyes were red from crying here in the privacy of her pod. To the others, she appeared calm, because she knew that's what they needed, but here in her room, she needed Jack.

And Jack was in terrible trouble.

She read the transcript again. These words from him were all she had now.

Message received. Plan in place. Nothing is what we thought. Don't come until you must. I will do all I can to make it safe. Mom, I'm doing what you taught me. I love you.

Fresh tears filled her eyes. Mom, I'm doing what you taught me. I love you.

The sentence was terrible and beautiful at once. Yes,

her sweet boy was doing what she had taught him, but she couldn't shake the fear that she'd sent him on an impossible mission that would end in an ugly death. Such an innocent boy, doing what she asked! What if she was mistaken about all of this?

Nothing is what we thought.

But what's happening, Jack? What were we wrong about?

He was alive, and for that she was grateful, but he was clearly in a predicament and was withholding information to protect her. Her dear, sweet boy was afraid she would be hurt if he told them what was really happening down there.

Captain Tillman was pushing for a descent to Earth in four days rather than six, because engineering had come up with a way to land safely, filter out toxins, and make good air in Earth's oxygen-rich atmosphere. As long as they stayed in the Arc, they would be safe.

But it was only a theory. And how long could they last, packed in the Arc like sardines?

Still, if they were going to die, it was better to die on Earth than in a tin can in space, the captain insisted. Only Michelle's demand that they wait the full seven days and this message from Jack had stopped him from giving the order to prepare for a launch.

Michelle set the message on the dresser and laid

down on the bed—the same bed Jack had often crawled into as a young boy when he was afraid.

She closed her eyes and tried to surrender to the great love, as she'd taught Jack. The love in which there was no fear. But that fear didn't leave her so quickly anymore.

She rolled over, pressed her face into the pillow, and began to sob.

CHAPTER FOUR

J ACK SAT under the large sloping boulder that formed the cave and glanced up at the morning sun. Still no sign of Camila, but it was early. Zeke was out there somewhere, hiding.

He'd built a small fire and watched it burn through the night, just in case predatory animals were around. He'd paced, stomach in knots, practicing the words he'd use when Camila showed up. If she showed up. If she didn't, he didn't know what he would do.

He'd tried to sleep but the ground was uncomfortable and his mind wouldn't slow down. The only way to convince Camila that the Reds didn't have her best interests in mind was to expose their lies. One significant lie was that Silvers were their enemies. If he could show her that Silvers posed no threat and in fact were the means of their salvation from the Reds, she would surely join him in his mission to kill the king.

She was following the Scaler way because it was all she knew, but she had a good heart—he'd seen it in her eyes when she brought dragon milk to him and Sammie. And she was curious. He had to get her to spend some time with Zeke. He'd never seen her with a dragon spear, so he hoped she would come unarmed.

He stood and scanned the clearing again. Birds chirped everywhere and the sun was growing hot. He was still alone.

What if she doesn't come at all? The single thought had plagued him all morning. Overwhelmed with it now, he stood and began pacing. With the space station running out of oxygen, he didn't have time for any new plans. Even if Camila agreed, they still had to track down the king and kill it! How long would that take?

Jack returned to the fire and nudged a smoldering log out of the pit so it would stop burning. No need for a fire now. He passed another slow hour in agony. Every time the wind rustled the bushes, Jack's heart surged. Was it Camila? Every time it wasn't, his desperation intensified. By midmorning, he was certain his plan had failed. For all he knew someone had thrown the note away without giving it to Camila. Maybe he should just go down there and speak to her in person. But the Village Mother had made it clear they would kill him if he returned. Even if they didn't kill him,

Zeke would never expose himself in the village. Nor could Jack persuade anyone to question their worship of the Reds in such a public setting.

He had to draw Camila out, alone.

He picked up a small steel cup sitting next to the fire, filled it with water from the pouch, and set the cup on the glowing embers. When he was little, nightmares would wake him. His mother would make him a cup of hot chocolate and hold him close. "Nothing can get you if your belly's full of hot chocolate," she would say. "It makes you too sweet."

He knew it wasn't true, but it always made him feel better. Right now he was glad he'd grabbed packs of chocolate powder from the Scalers' shuttle stash. He had one left. His mind drifted to his mother's face as he waited for the water to heat up. He wished he could talk to her now. She would know what to do.

"Hello, boy from the stars."

Jack snapped his head up to see a familiar face. But not the face he'd hoped to see.

Lukas stood alone fifteen feet away, his shoulders broad and his expression dark. Lukas? Of all the scenarios Jack had played in his mind, this wasn't one of them.

Jack stood, his body tense. A long dragon spear was slung across Lukas's back. The last time Jack had seen him, the dragon hunter was gloating with Tichondrius at his feet, threatening to kill Jack. What if he'd come to make good on his threat?

Lukas raised his hands in a sign of surrender. "I haven't come to harm you. I'm sorry I threatened you last time we met." He shrugged and lowered his hands. "Though you did deserve it, taking up with those Silvers."

So he isn't sorry, Jack thought. He just wants to appear sorry. Why?

"Are you alone?" Jack asked.

"Do I look like I need backup?" Lukas grinned.

"You didn't answer my question."

"I'm alone. Are you?" He held Jack's gaze. Jack knew Lukas wouldn't hesitate to kill Zeke given the chance.

"Yes," Jack said.

Lukas gave a nod. "Good, then it's just us."

"Where's Camila?"

Lukas ignored his question. "What is this information you have on the Silvers?"

"It's information I'll give only to Camila. That's why I asked her to come."

"You don't just summon a queen-to-be," Lukas said. "She summons you. If you want to speak with my sister, you'll have to return to the village with me."

"Your mother threatened to kill me if I ever returned," Jack said.

"Yes, but things have changed," Lukas said. He took a few steps. "Your friend Sammie has returned and convinced the Village Mother that killing you would be a mistake. She's a true Scaler now, by the way."

Jack's heart stopped at the mention of Sammie. So she was alive! When he'd learned that only a redeemed one could kill the dragon king, Jack's first thought had been Sammie. She had just recently turned and they had a shared history. But he'd already tried and failed to save her. She'd already heard the truth of love from him and rejected it.

So why would she convince the Village Mother not to kill him? Maybe even in her delusion Sammie still cared for him. Pain nipped at his chest. He was doing this for her as much as for his mother. Maybe he could go back to the village and talk with her. Maybe she could be the redeemed one after all.

He shut the fleeting thought down as quickly as it had risen. He could feel his desperation growing like a low hum in his gut. He didn't have time for all that. The Sanctuary didn't have time.

"If you would like to speak with Camila and see your friend Sammie, all you have to do is return to the village with me," Lukas said, yanking Jack from his thoughts.

Jack's mind buzzed. What if Lukas was only luring him into a trap?

A terrifying thought filled his mind. Lukas was the last Scaler he would have picked to persuade, but he was here now, and Zeke was close by. Who better to kill the dragon king than Lukas?

First he had to outsmart the dragon hunter.

"I'm not sure I can trust any of you," Jack said.

"Not even your friend from the stars?" Lukas questioned.

"She's different now."

"Because she's a Scaler? Because she finally sees the truth?"

"Sammie sees what she thinks is truth, but she saw something different before. Who's to say that wasn't the truth?"

Lukas crossed his arms and huffed. "There's only one truth: serve the Reds or die."

Jack felt his fear easing. "I don't serve the Reds and I'm not dead."

"Only because you're immune. A freak of nature."

"Or maybe because I follow a different path," Jack said. "At least hear me out. What if you could become immune yourself?"

Lukas opened his mouth and then paused. Excitement pricked Jack's brain. Maybe he really could help Lukas see reason.

"History and time," Lukas said a second later. "That's what makes me think I'm on the right path."

"You're under the control of the Reds," Jack dared point out.

Lukas's eyes flared and Jack knew he'd struck a nerve.

"When the Silvers offered you another way, did you even try?" Jack said, knowing he was in dangerous territory,

Lukas's shoulders tensed and his hands balled. For a second Jack thought Lukas might charge him, but then Lukas relaxed.

"Their way is death," Lukas said.

"What if I could show you that's also a lie?" Jack asked. "I was with the Silvers and I'm alive, aren't I? If I could show you the Silvers mean you no harm—"

"I'll never fall for the trickery of those monsters!" Lukas snapped. He spit to the side, anger flashing in his eyes. "Never!"

Jack knew then that Lukas was far too deceived by so many years of following the Reds' path of fear. He would never consider new ideas. If Zeke showed up now, Lukas would bury his spear in the Silver's throat.

Like a flame sparked in the dead of night, an idea flashed through Jack's mind. What if he could disarm and disable Lukas? If he could subdue the warrior, maybe he could get him to listen to Zeke long enough to hear the dragon without putting Zeke in harm's way.

"You're a fool to listen to their lies, boy," Lukas said.

Jack remembered the dragon sleep flower in his pocket. What if he used it on Lukas? But of course! He had to try.

Lukas wasn't finished. "Sammie assures us that you'll see reason, but I'm thinking she's wrong."

"Not necessarily," Jack said. He paced and sighed. "Maybe I am following a fool's path."

Lukas eyed Jack curiously. "The first reasonable thing you've said."

Keep thinking that, Jack thought. He needed Lukas to think he might be changing course enough to lower his guard.

Jack turned to the smoldering fire. With his back to Lukas, he slipped his hand into his pocket and carefully removed one of the petals from the dragon sleep flower. "Earth is different than I thought it'd be," he said. "I don't know where I belong anymore."

"All people belong with the Reds," Lukas said, the tension gone from his voice. "If you submit, we Scalers will welcome you as one of our own."

Jack glanced over his shoulder to see the boy approaching the firepit. He had to hurry! He smashed the petal in his fingers as best he could, knelt, and dropped the dragon sleep into the cup of hot water.

Hand trembling slightly, Jack pulled the last packet of chocolate powder from his pack, then stood and tore it open, facing Lukas, who was now only three paces away.

"If I return with you, will I get to see Sammie?" Jack baited.

"Yes," Lukas said, eyes on the chocolate packet. "You feel deeply for her?" He lifted his eyes and winked. "Someday you might make her yours. If you join us, that is."

That wasn't how Jack saw Sammie. "She's my closest friend. My only friend, really. I'm alone without her."

Lukas nodded as if he understood. "Come with me and you'll never be alone again. We'll be your tribe."

Jack felt a pulse of guilt. It felt strange to manipulate Lukas. But his mother's life depended on his success. Besides, Lukas was clearly trying to manipulate him into returning to the village.

"I've never had a real tribe," Jack said. He emptied the packet of chocolate into the cup, covering the flower petals. The smell of chocolate wafted into the air.

"I recognize that smell," Lukas said. "What is that?"

"Hot chocolate," Jack answered.

Lukas's eyes lit up. "Chocolate. Like the bars I recovered from your ship?"

"It's the same, only you drink it," Jack said, stirring the mix with a stick. "It's a small comfort. Better than the bar you ate, I think."

He lifted the hot cup and sniffed the brown liquid. Then tilted it and pretended to take a sip. Thankfully, none of the crushed petal had risen to the top.

Lukas glanced at the cup cautiously and then back at Jack. "We must find a way to make this drink in the village."

"All you need is a cacao tree. I'm sure it can be found around somewhere." He pretended to take another sip, then held the cup out. "Here, give it a try."

Lukas stepped forward and took the cup. Jack's heart quickened as Lukas raised the cup to his lips and sipped the liquid. The older boy smiled as the hot chocolate drained down his throat.

"It's quite delicious," Lukas said. "I've never known such a thing." He took another large gulp and handed the cup out.

Had he taken enough? Zeke had said that even a small amount would put a human to sleep. Still, he had to make sure this worked.

"You can have more," Jack said.

"I can't take all your warm chocolate," Lukas said.

Jack swallowed nervously and shook his head. "I don't mind. I already had some."

Lukas eyes him curiously. "Then why make more?"

Jack searched for a good lie as suspicion wrinkled Lukas's brow. But it was too late. Lukas could sense foul play. He tossed the contents of the cup on the ground and turned back with a fiery expression.

For a brief second, Jack thought he was done for, but before Lukas could take a full step toward him his expression changed. He swayed slightly and looked at Jack with concern.

"What did you . . ."

Lukas's question trailed off and he tried to take a step, but the dragon sleep was swimming through his body. He staggered.

"You . . ." Lukas tried to lunge for him but he was already too far gone. He managed only two steps before falling to his knees. Dust lifted into the air as he collapsed face first onto the dirt and went still.

Jack stared down at the fallen hunter. It had worked! He dared to poke Lukas's body with the toe of his boot. The boy didn't budge.

Jack released the breath he'd been holding.

It was time for Zeke.

CHAPTER FIVE

LUKAS HADN'T moved a muscle in well over an hour. Jack secured his hands and feet with rope and then dragged his body out of the sun into the shelter of the small cave. His plan was simple and required Zeke, but he didn't want to call Zeke in before Lukas stirred. The less time Zeke remained in the clearing, the less likely he would be discovered.

Jack watched Lukas's chest rise and fall with his even breathing. The Scaler was propped against the wall, hands secure behind his back, legs extended forward, ankles tied together. He was harmless in sleep, but that wouldn't last long.

He didn't have time for Lukas to be unconscious all day. So he adapted his plan to speed things up.

He filled a water pouch at a small stream close to the cave and took it back to Lukas. Jack hesitated to disturb the sleeping giant. He had no idea what would happen once he roused Lukas, but time was ticking by quickly.

Jack uncorked the water pouch, took a deep breath, tossed some of the icy cold water on Lukas's face, and jumped back into the sunlight.

Now, Zeke! he thought, knowing Zeke would hear his mind. Come now! Hurry!

"In a flash, Jack," came the Silver's carefree response.

Lukas lay still for a moment, then sputtered to life, gasping and coughing. His eyes blinked open.

"Where . . . ?" He closed his mouth, clearly disoriented.

Jack stood back, waiting for reality to crash into Lukas. The warrior looked around, clicked quickly under his tongue to define the space, then turned to Jack. His eyes narrowed to slits as he recovered his memory.

Lukas grunted and tried to lurch forward, only then realizing he was bound. He glanced at the twine around his ankles and looked up. Deep resentment poured from his milky eyeballs, enough to frighten Jack.

"What have you done?" Lukas growled.

"I needed you to listen to me and I'm running out of options," Jack said.

"How did you manage this?" Lukas barked. "What did you do to me?"

"I gave you dragon sleep. It was in the hot chocolate."

Lukas's eyes widened again. "You tricked me."

"You wouldn't have listened otherwise. And I couldn't risk you putting anyone in danger."

"Well, you're in danger now, fool," Lukas bit off.

"Hear me out—"

"I will do nothing you ask! You drugged me against my will. Release me immediately!"

"I can't do that. You have to listen to me!"

"When I get out of these restraints . . ." Lukas started. But then he took several deep breaths and something shifted behind his eyes. Maybe he saw the hopelessness of his predicament. Lukas relaxed, keeping his milky eyes glued to Jack.

"This is a foolish mistake," he finally said. "But if you release me, I promise not to harm you or mention the incident. It's an embarrassment for both of us."

"I can't release you yet," Jack said.

"Of course you can," Lukas snapped. "What you mean is that you won't. Fine. Then tell me what to do to earn my freedom." Jack was aware the Scaler would try to trick him, but he hadn't met Zeke yet.

Jack glanced at the sky. Still no sign of the Silver.

He looked at Lukas. "I'll cut you free when you've heard and considered the truth," he said.

"And what truth is that?"

"That the Reds lied to you about the Silvers."

Anger flashed across Lukas's face. "What will that accomplish?"

"If you see that the Reds lied to you about the Silvers, then maybe you'll consider they've lied to you about everything else."

"You really think tying me up will convince me to hear what I've already heard?"

"But what if I can show you it's true?" Jack took a step forward. "What if you could be free from your blindness? From the scales that cover your skin? Free from your fear? Wouldn't you want that?"

Lukas hesitated, considering. "Fear is good. It is the beginning of wisdom. Why would I want to be free from it?"

"Because it keeps you enslaved to the Reds and lost in a world of suffering. It blinds you to the way of love. A way beyond fear. The way of Yeshua."

The dragon hunter looked up at him curiously for a few beats.

"Such strange words. What have the Silvers done to you?"

"They reminded me of what my mother taught me before I came to Earth. That there are only two ways in this world: the way of fear and the way of love. You can't serve two masters. In every moment you choose which to follow. The way of fear blinds you to love, but the path of love sets you free from fear."

"That way leads to death," Lukas said.

"No," Jack replied. "It leads to true life."

Lukas let Jack's words sink in, then shook his head. "No, the things you say make no sense."

Jack exhaled, trying not to be frustrated. Maybe he wasn't saying them correctly. Where was Zeke?

As if on cue, a great shadow blocked the sun for a moment, then Zeke landed heavily to Jack's right, still out of Lukas's line of sight.

Lukas jerked up, nerves on edge. "What is that?"

Jack took a calming breath. "I want you to meet someone," he said. "Just listen to what he has to say." Then he turned and nodded at Zeke, who was watching him eagerly, like a huge pet ready for his treat.

But Zeke was no pet. He was a Silver who knew no fear, because he lived in love, and there was no fear in love. He would gladly give his life to rescue even one soul from the fear that ruled this world.

The mighty young beast thumped forward and came into full view of the shallow cave.

Lukas clicked frantically and his face paled. He was afraid, Jack realized. Lukas yanked his knees to his chest and pressed his back into the wall.

It wasn't the reaction Jack had expected from

the warrior, but then he recalled what Zevonus had said. Reds were terrified of Silvers. Fear was afraid of love, because love revealed fear for what it really was: powerless.

"Lukas," he said softly. "This is Zeke."

Zeke bowed his head, and Jack waited for the dragon to meld with Lukas and reveal his truths. If Lukas could hear Zeke, could feel his peace and love, then surely Lukas would question his beliefs. The Scaler, even in deception, was too smart to ignore what was right in front of him. Right?

Lukas seemed to have lost his voice. This is going to work, Jack thought.

Zeke's voice echoed in Jack's mind. "I can't meld with him, young Jack," the Silver said. "His mind and heart are blocked."

"What?" Jack said out loud, jerking his head up to look at Zeke. "You can't just force your way in?'

"I can only meld with those who are open and willing. Love never forces itself on anyone. It casts out fear, but only when someone is willing to align to it. In my experience, most humans are terrified of true love. It's what led to the great religious wars that destroyed this world."

Zeke's voice was calm, but Jack's mind raced with fear.

"You have to do something to make him open up to you!" Jack cried. Desperation crawled under his skin like ants.

"I cannot," Zeke said. "Only he can choose."

"We have to try! He will listen to you, I know it."

"How dare you bring this monster before me," Lukas hissed. "I will slay the foul beast where he stands."

"You have to stop blocking him," Jack pleaded with Lukas. "You have to let him meld with you."

Lukas looked as if Jack had just suggested he jump off a cliff to his death. "Never."

"I am sorry, young Jack," Zeke said to him. "But there is nothing I can do."

The Silver bowed to Lukas even as the warrior raged. Undisturbed, Zeke turned to leave.

"Where are you going?" Jack asked, following him out of Lukas's line of sight. "Zeke, please! I know love doesn't force, but you have to do something! I'm running out of time."

"I believe the rest of this journey may be yours alone, young Jack," Zeke said.

"What does that mean?"

"It means he has rejected me. Showing him the way is your path now."

"So you're just leaving me?"

"We are always close, young Jack. But my presence

will only interfere with his ability to hear you. You are the one they will listen to."

Zevonus had said there would come a point when he'd have to move on alone, but he'd never imagined that time would come so quickly. He'd barely started! And everything he'd planned so far had gone sideways.

Zeke's bright blue eyes offered courage. "You can do this, young Jack. Remember who you are, light-bringer, and the way will become clear."

Jack clasped the ring Zevonus had given him, the one that hung around his neck, and searched his mind for the small, still voice of his mother. Zeke lowered his head. Jack placed his forehead against the dragon's scaled brow, swallowing the lump in his throat.

He could feel Zeke's love and peace and it filled him with warmth. Then the dragon pulled away and, with a final nod toward Jack, lifted into the sky.

Jack watched until he could no longer see the dragon, feeling lost and alone.

He walked back to the cave and stared at Lukas, trying his best to release the fear gathered in his chest. Zeke's words floated through his mind. You are the one they will listen to. But Lukas wasn't listening. If Jack had days, maybe he could get the boy to see, but they didn't have days. Not even hours, because others would start searching for Lukas.

You are the one. Zeke's words played in his mind. What if Jack used his blood on Lukas as he had with Sammie? Maybe that's what Zeke had meant, that only Jack's blood could help the Scalers hear the truth. He'd hoped to avoid such desperation, but everything he was doing was desperate. And that's why he'd recovered the pack with the blood kit in it, right?

He wasn't sure how a long-time Scaler would react to his blood, but he was out of options. And running out of time.

"Where did the Silver go?" Lukas asked in a frail voice.

Jack needed to play this correctly. He couldn't force Lukas to take his blood. The warrior was tied, but he could still move his arms with ease. Jack needed to find a way to get Lukas to take his blood willingly.

"I sent him away because you seemed so afraid of him," Jack said, allowing himself the half lie.

"I'm not afraid of any Silver," Lukas spat.

"Really? That's not how it looked to me."

"I've killed many Silvers! Why would I be afraid of them?"

"I know you've killed many. You have seven silver rings on your bicep to prove it."

"Eight," Lukas corrected. "I still need to mold one for the Silver I killed on the high plateau."

Tichondrius.

"Either way, you were afraid," Jack pushed.

"You read me wrong, foolish boy," Lukas said.

"But I'm not wrong. Fear always attacks the truth that exposes how powerless fear is."

"How dare you say I'm powerless?!"

"You've given all your power to the Reds."

Lukas sneered at Jack. "I kill dragons with a single spear."

"As commanded by the Reds. You're a puppet." Jack was tired of trying to be tricky.

"Nobody tells me what to do!" Lukas snapped.

Jack opened the pack that rested against the stone and pulled out the medical supplies he'd need. "From where I'm standing, it looks like every move you make is commanded by someone else. The Reds, your older sister, the Village Mother. They say jump and you say how high."

"Careful," Lukas growled.

Jack tied off his own arm, found a vein and inserted the tip of a long needle. Blood filled the syringe as he spoke. "If I'm wrong, then prove it." Jack removed the needle, then stepped up to Lukas, syringe in hand.

"I don't have to prove anything to you," Lukas objected.

"Because you're afraid?" Jack said. "I think you're afraid that I might be right about the Reds. I think you don't want to know the truth, because then you'd have to admit you really are a puppet."

Lukas frowned. "I'm not afraid of being wrong because I am not wrong. You're the blind one."

"Let's put it to the test then," Jack said. He dropped to a squat, Lukas's milky eyes watching him through their fog. He held up the syringe filled with his blood.

"What's that?" Lukas asked.

"This is my blood. I gave it to Sammie in the village and it cured her of the effects of dragon milk because I'm immune. Right before your mother banished us."

"Now you want to give it to me, is that it?"

"Do you wanna see if you're a puppet?" Jack asked. He watched Lukas eye the syringe cautiously as though it were full of poison. "Or are you afraid of that too?"

The wheels behind Lukas's eyes were turning. Jack could feel him weighing his options, thinking through the best move.

"It's just a little blood."

That gave the Scaler pause.

"Fine," Lukas said. "Give me your blood and I'll show you how powerless you are."

Surprised, Jack didn't wait for Lukas to change his

mind. He found a vein on the Scaler's arm. "It might sting but it won't harm you." Lukas didn't flinch as the needle pricked his skin or as the blood filled his vein.

Satisfied, Jack withdrew the needle and took a deep breath. "See? It's nothing."

"Of course it's nothing. Because you are nothing."

Jack returned the syringe to the pack without reacting to the cutting words. Then he sat down five feet from the Scaler and crossed his legs.

"Now what?" Lukas asked.

"Now we wait to see if you come to your senses," Jack said.

Lukas harrumphed. "No need to wait. I came to my senses a long time ago."

Then they said nothing.

The day was hot and the birds went about their business from tree to tree. Jack watched Lukas's eyes for a sign of clearing. Or any sign at all that his blood had some effect on the lifelong Scaler.

Over a minute passed. Jack was beginning to think the transfusion had failed when Lukas clamped his eyes shut and groaned. He gritted his teeth and jerked his head back, clearly in pain.

Jack's heart bolted. Something was happening, but Sammie hadn't reacted this way. A terrible thought crowded his mind.

What if his blood killed Lukas?

CHAPTER SIX

L UKAS WAS reacting to Jack's blood—either that or faking it, which Jack doubted. Sweat beaded the Scaler's forehead and his face was red.

The dragon hunter went stiff, grinding his teeth, then collapsed like a limp rag, hands and feet still bound. Jack reminded himself to breathe as he waited for Lukas to move, but the Scaler looked like he was in a deep sleep. He was breathing, so he wasn't dead. That was a start.

Jack crept forward and dared to poke Lukas's shoulder. "Lukas?"

The older boy jerked at the sound of his voice, slowly lifted his head, and opened his eyes. They were still milky. Sammie's eyes had always cleared after taking his blood.

Did his blood not work on a lifelong Scaler? That couldn't be! He didn't have a plan C! The shallow cave felt suffocating, and he couldn't breathe in the stuffy air.

He stumbled into the sunlight and inhaled the cool mountain breeze. He knew freaking out wouldn't help the situation, but his mother's life depended on him finding a way to redeem a Scaler. And they still had to kill the dragon king.

It was hopeless!

"What's happening to me?" Lukas whimpered.

Jack turned and was struck by the confusion on Lukas's face.

His milky eyes were wide. "Something's wrong with me."

Jack stepped back into the shallow cave, watching Lukas carefully. "What do you mean?"

Lukas swallowed and shook his head. "I . . . I don't know."

A spark of hope ignited in Jack's mind. He dropped to one knee and laid a comforting hand on the older boy's knee. "It's alright. Take your time."

Lukas's face twisted with remorse. "I feel terrible," he whispered.

"You're ill? Maybe that will pass."

"No, not that."

"Then what?" Jack asked.

"I . . . I feel terrible for killing the Silver in the field."

Jack straightened, still on one knee. "Tichondrius?"

Lukas looked up at him. "He had a name?"

"They all have names. Don't the Reds have names?"

Lukas shrugged. "I don't know. That's not the kind of relationship we have with the dragons."

Jack's hope soared. Lukas was seeing the world in a new light. He remembered that Sammie had felt terrible about all the things she'd done under the influence of dragon toxin. Jack wasn't sure how it all worked, but he knew Lukas was experiencing something new.

"What is happening to me?" Lukas asked again, more urgently.

"I think my blood's helping you see things differently," Jack said.

"Like it did with Sammie," Lukas said.

"Yes. Different, but you're different."

Lukas was staring at Jack's chin, in deep thought. "Maybe your blood is deceiving me."

"Is that how it feels?"

Lukas hesitated, then swallowed deeply. "No."

"How does it feel?"

"Like maybe I was tricked into believing something that isn't true?"

"Tricked by whom?" Jack pressed, barely breathing again.

Lukas hesitated a long beat. "The Reds," he said.

"Because you were tricked!" Jack blurted. "The Reds and their queens made you believe you needed to embrace fear of them to be safe, but it's the opposite."

For a long moment, Lukas stared past Jack to the open sky beyond the shallow cave.

"I feel betrayed," Lukas finally said. "Like I was a fool to give my life to a lie."

Waves of relief washed over Jack. It was working!

"You can't blame yourself. Everyone on Earth is blinded by fear, even me. It's the same fear that killed billions in the religious wars. But we can see beyond fear to a new way of being. That's what I'm doing. It's our only hope."

"I can still feel the pull of the Reds, calling me back," Lukas said.

"Don't listen!" Jack cried. "You can hear another voice, a still, quiet voice that will guide you through the darkness. The voice of Yeshua."

"Who?"

"Yeshua."

"I know nothing of Yeshua."

"My mother taught me his teachings," Jack said. "If you want, I can teach you."

"And this Yeshua offers freedom?" Lukas asked.

Jack smiled. "Yes. His way leads us into a love beyond fear, because there is no fear in love."

"I am afraid all the time," Lukas whispered. "I don't even know what it would be like to never know fear."

"Because you haven't embraced love. True love cannot be provoked and holds no record of wrong."

"You know this love?" the Scaler asked.

"I have. I do when I surrender to it, but I'm still on my journey to discover it myself. I know it's the way of Yeshua and I believe in him, but I still haven't fully embraced love. Like I said, that's what I'm here to learn."

Clarity filled Jack's mind. Everything became plain. All of this was as much for his sake as the Scalers. He was going through the same process as Lukas. He knew about real love, but it still wasn't his way of being.

"What about my people?" Lukas said. "I can't just abandon them."

"We won't. We'll come back for—"

"Back?" Lukas interrupted. "No, we must go to them now!" Lukas sat up as best he could. He struggled against the ties that bound his wrists and ankles. "Release me from these."

Jack pulled back a bit, his suspicions rising. "I don't think—"

"If what you say is true and the Reds have been lying to us, then I have to tell my people! Help me show them, Jack," Lukas said.

Warning bells were sounding in Jack's mind. If he

released Lukas, the boy could easily overpower him. What if it was all a ploy to get Jack to release him? Could he trust Lukas?

"I understand you don't trust me," Lukas said. "After all I've done . . ." the older boy's words trailed off and he hung his head in shame.

"I'm not saying I don't trust you," Jack said softly. "I'm just not sure you see as clearly as—"

"But I do see! I see how fear is a lie, and I see we have been worshiping that lie, which has bound us to the Reds. They rule our hearts and we can waste no time in setting the others free! Sammie told us of your plan to kill the queens. I see now that it's the only way to destroy the hives, but we need help!"

Lukas's mention of the queens surprised Jack. That had been the plan before Jack learned about the dragon king. He'd forgotten the Scalers weren't aware of a dragon king. A small voice told Jack there was no reason to share that information until he was absolutely certain.

Lukas settled a little. "I just can't stop thinking about all the lies, all the times I put my trust in the queens' ways. Even now, as I feel their call to obey, their manipulation runs deep. It has to end!"

He looked at Jack, face pleading.

"Come back to the village with me. Speak with my

mother. Give her your blood. Let her feel what I'm feeling now, and she won't be able to ignore the truth."

"We will go back to the village, but first you and I will kill the queen here. I have poisoned arrows filled with toxin made from my blood."

Lukas pondered this. "We could try, but I know the Reds well. If you think we can approach their hive without a major distraction, you're wrong."

"I have gas that will put them to sleep," Jack said.

"And you know this will work? How? The Reds aren't like other creatures. If your gas fails, then we're finished. No, we must have help! Trust me, I know this."

Jack wanted to believe him, but had his blood really changed the warrior so quickly? Then again, wasn't that how truth often worked? It only took a small perspective shift to see the light. If his blood had so easily helped Lukas see, wouldn't it do the same with the Village Mother?

If they had the help of many redeemed Scalers, then they could surely destroy the dragon king.

But what if the effects of his blood wore off, as it had with Sammie?

When they stopped drinking the milk, dragon toxin would make them sick. He would have to give those who hunted the queen his blood, but how much could he spare?

There was so much he didn't know and couldn't plan for. It was like walking into the dark without any sense of direction. But what else could he do?

"Please, Jack," Lukas pleaded. "Look at me. What I say is true. I've always been a seeker of truth. All of my life I've been told there's only one way. I would have died for that truth, but now I can see something else. A different path. My mother has a good heart, as do we all. I know they will see it as well. Help us, so we can end this madness!"

His eyes were still milky, but his words felt so authentic. Despite his reservations, Jack knew he was going to trust Lukas. He needed him to defeat the dragon king.

"Just undo my ankles so I can walk," Lukas said. "I have no need for my hands."

Jack took a deep breath and released the Scaler's ankles. Lukas struggled to his feet. A smile lit his face and Jack braced for the worst. But the older boy made no attempt to free his hands or attack him.

"Let's go," Lukas said. "We must give the Village Mother your blood before the evening ceremony." Lukas walked into the sunlight.

Jack hesitated.

Lukas turned back around, clicking softly. "What are you waiting for?"

"Are you sure your mother will be able to see the truth?" Jack asked.

"I did, didn't I?" Lukas said. "And you'll have my protection. No one will harm you. I swear it."

As they walked through the forest to the village, Jack told Lukas stories of Yeshua. Lukas listened intently and asked questions, doing his best to understand the teachings. The longer they talked, the more confident Jack felt. Lukas was a quick learner, and others might be as well. Especially Camila, destined to be the next Village Mother. Maybe this really was the best way to end the dragon king's rule.

He still didn't know where the dragon king was or how they would defeat him, but he was eager to share a few ideas with Lukas when the time was right.

Lukas stopped and faced Jack as they neared the village. "We're close. I'm not sure walking in with my hands bound will serve you. It will make people think you are the enemy, and you aren't."

Jack nodded and untied the rope around Lukas's wrists. The older boy rubbed the red marks on his wrists and guilt blossomed in Jack's chest.

Lukas noticed. "Don't worry, Jack. I would have

bound you too." He threw Jack a wink and headed on through the dense forest. Jack's heart raced as the first signs of the village came into view. He said a short prayer for strength under his breath and followed Lukas into the village clearing.

Heads raised as the boys approached the outer huts. Soft whispers spread as more and more eyes moved to see them. Giggling children played in a circle near a small hut. He hardly remembered there being children. It was strange to see scaled, white-eyed humans so small and innocent.

He smiled at a girl no older than five who broke from the group and skipped up to him, clicking softly. She stopped in front of Jack and grinned.

"You're the one they're waiting for?" the little girl asked.

A woman emerged from the hut. "Myra! Get yourself back here right this moment!" With a giggle, little Myra bounced away as her mother demanded.

Jack's mind raced. They've been waiting for me? Something wasn't right.

He suddenly wanted to run back into the forest, away from this place. But he had come too far now.

Ahead, the dragon totem towered over the village. As Jack watched, Camila and the Village Mother approached him, followed by a trio of guards. Jack slowed as he made eye contact with the Village Mother. His memory of her death threat sent a ripple down his spine.

Lukas grabbed Jack's wrist and yanked him forward, nearly jerking him off his feet. The kindness in the dragon hunter's face was gone, and Jack knew he'd been played.

"Did you really think your blood could affect me?" Lukas asked, dragging him toward the women. "Stupid Jack. My loyalty to the Reds runs deeper than blood."

Lukas pushed Jack toward the Village Mother, then stood at his back to ensure he couldn't run. "As promised, I present the little fool who conspires with our enemy," he announced.

Jack opened his mouth but nothing came out. Camila was looking at him with a flat expression, but she wasn't scowling. He still thought she would have heard him out. But it was too late now.

"Welcome back, boy from the stars," the Village Mother said.

"So, what now?" Jack asked. "You're just going to kill me?"

"Fortunately for you, things have changed," the Village Mother said. "Sammie is very convincing."

Sammie! "Where is she?"

"Come with me," the Village Mother said, turning toward a hut.

Heart in his throat, Jack followed Camila and the Village Mother willingly, surrounded by the guards and a gloating Lukas, who had played his part all too well.

The hut was larger than the others, and a thick leather hide hung over the entrance, serving as a door. A guard pulled the hide back. The Village Mother motioned for Jack to enter. "We will give you a moment with Sammie."

Jack hesitated, then, with a push from Lukas, stumbled into the hut. The leather flap closed behind him, cutting off the sunlight. It took a moment for Jack's eyes to adjust to the dimness.

"Hi, Jack," a warm, familiar voice said.

Sammie stepped out of the shadows. Scales covered her arms, and her dark braided hair was pulled back from her face, painted like Camila's. Her eyes were milky and she wore leathered garb.

She was a Scaler. He'd known this, but seeing made it real.

Emotion clutched his throat. "Sammie," he said. They stood in silence for a moment and then she rushed forward and wrapped her arms around his neck. He hadn't expected the sudden embrace and stood frozen for a moment. But her warmth settled him and he wrapped his arms around her. He could feel her scales, but he didn't care. He'd missed her so badly.

"I'm so glad you came," Sammie said.

"I was tricked into coming," Jack said.

Sammie pulled back and lowered her arms. "Don't be upset. He was doing it for me."

"For you?" Jack asked. "Why?"

"I couldn't stand the idea of leaving you out there alone," she said. "I know you don't see things the way we do, but I also know how smart you are. It isn't safe out there. At least in here you'll be protected until you decide to join us."

He had no intention of joining them, but saying so wouldn't help. So he shifted her attention to something he thought she might care about.

"Things have gotten much worse on the Sanctuary, Sammie. They're running out of oxygen. They're preparing the Arc for a descent to Earth in six days. We have to make Earth safe for our families or they'll all die. We're running out of time!"

Sammie stepped back. "But Earth isn't safe, Jack. And the Scalers are also my family."

His heart sank.

"Do you really want the rest of your family to end up slaves to the Reds?"

She narrowed her eyes. "I want my family to be safe and alive. I want everyone to be together. It's good they're coming. The Scalers will let them join, and we can be one people."

"There's another way, Sammie!" Jack said, reaching for her hands. She snatched them away and took a step back.

"Enough is enough, Jack. There is no other way! Surely you can see that by now."

He pressed in, desperate to bring her to her senses. "I learned some things from the Silvers, things that change everything."

"What things?"

He wasn't sure how much to tell her. But it didn't matter, because in the next moment, someone pulled open the leather hide, and the Village Mother walked in with Camila.

"Yes, what things?" the Village Mother demanded. "What lies have poisoned your mind?"

Jack looked from the Village Mother to Camila, then back to Sammie. It would have been one thing to talk to Sammie, but he couldn't disclose anything to the Village Mother.

"Have you nothing to say?" the Village Mother pressed.

Sammie stared at him without a shred of concern. She really was completely lost.

"Village Mother," Camila said softly. "Perhaps I could have a moment with Jack."

She gave her daughter a nod. "Very well. Please talk some sense into him."

She motioned for Sammie to follow her out. Sammie paused at his side. "I just want you to be safe, Jack," she whispered. Then they were gone.

Silence filled the hut as Jack tried to still his aching heart. He was sure Sammie was beyond reach. That left only Camila.

Jack looked at her eyeing him kindly.

"I'm sorry my brother tricked you," Camila said. "I hoped he'd find a way to bring you without resorting to manipulation, but I have long given up trying to control my brother."

"Why didn't you come yourself?" he asked.

"That was decided by my mother," Camila answered. "For my safety."

"I would never hurt you."

"No?" Camila tilted her head. "Did you not have a Silver with you?"

Jack opened his mouth to respond and then closed it. Lukas must have told them everything.

"What was your plan, Jack?" Camila asked. "Do you actually have information about the Silvers for me? Or were you just trying to get me out there alone?"

"I was hoping to show you that the Silvers aren't what you think."

Camila's eyes darkened. "And you thought I would listen?"

"You've been kind to me," Jack said.

"You mistake my kindness for weakness then," Camila said, her tongue sharp.

"I just thought you'd be open—"

"You were wrong, boy from the stars."

She sounded like the Village Mother. The last of Jack's hope died.

"I'm more committed to my people than you understand. I would never follow you down a path that leads to their destruction. You have miscalculated." Each word felt like a nail to his heart. He felt stupid for being so naïve. Foolish boy from the stars.

"It was a mistake to let you leave before," Camila said. "You will stay here, under careful watch, until you see reason. Sammie still believes you can be saved. Though I have my doubts, time will tell."

Jack felt his entire world crash down around him. He'd failed his mother.

"Please try to understand that even with all you have done, we simply want the best for you," Camila said, voice soft again. "But make no mistake, the best way is our way. I hope for your sake you can see that, Jack."

Jack wanted to say something—anything to confirm even a sliver of hope that Camila could be redeemed. But nothing came to mind. His blood didn't work on lifelong Scalers. They were blind in sight and heart, and he didn't know how to help them see.

"You and I will speak more later," Camila said. "For now you should rest and think about what I've said. Please don't try to leave. There's no reason for you to make this harder than it needs to be."

Camila left, and Jack found himself alone in the dim hut, weighed down by the crushing blow of failure. He stumbled to the single sleeping mat at the back of the hut and collapsed in tears. With his face pressed into the soft mat, he prayed to see light in the darkness that was pressing in on all sides.

But even now the light was fading.

CHAPTER SEVEN

LUKAS CAME for Jack about two hours later, although he'd lost track of time in the dark place, so it might have been one hour or three. The dragon hunter escorted him to a hut high in the trees. Two guards would ensure he stayed put during the evening ceremony. He'd declined their invitation to attend and asked to see Sammie, but Lukas had only huffed.

Jack guessed they wanted him to watch the ceremony, because he had a perfect view of the dragon altar from above. They really do hope to convert me, he thought.

The sun was almost down. He watched them pile wood for the fire under the towering dragon totem. The dread of crushing defeat consumed him. He couldn't see how to bring any Scaler from the darkness to the light in time to defeat the dragon king before the Sanctuary returned to Earth. He'd really believed it was possible, but he saw now how foolish that thought had been.

The Reds had blinded each and every one of them to the truth of love in the light. No wonder the Silvers had failed to bring the truth. He'd been a fool and everyone he loved would pay for it. The residents of the Sanctuary would come to Earth and drink dragon milk to become Scalers, or die. Sitting above the Scaler village, his legs dangling off the wooden ledge that wrapped around the tree house, all Jack could think about was his mother. He couldn't imagine her as a Scaler. She would give up her life before drinking the milk.

And so would he. Or would he? A desperate idea had nipped at his mind a few times, but he refused to dwell on it.

The fire was soon raging. Scalers gathered around it and let out a thunderous whoop that drew Jack's attention. Lukas strode to the center of the circle, his shoulders back, chin raised. Following him, two Scalers carried a large sack.

Lukas stepped forward, his bloody spear raised high as the warriors dumped the object out of the sack onto the altar. "Today I have slain another of our enemy. An enemy who tried to undermine my loyalty to the queen!"

The crowd roared with approval and Jack saw the object was a huge eyeball. Surely taken from a dragon. His heart began to race.

Lukas turned his head so that he was staring up and across the village directly at Jack. "The Silver they call Zeke!" he cried.

Again the Scalers cheered into the dark sky. Jack's heart broke. How had Lukas so quickly tracked down and killed Zeke? The Silver must have stayed close to keep an eye out for him and been surprised. First Tichondrius and now Zeke. Two beautiful souls lost because of him. Jack was too numb to cry.

A terrible darkness swallowed him as he watched the Village Mother congratulate her son and then begin their nightly ritual. They left Zeke's eye on the altar as they began. They'd taken the young Silver's eye, but in truth, they were the blind ones. Far too blind to redeem, he thought bitterly.

So many years of obedience to fear couldn't be undone quickly. The thought that had picked at his brain returned, and this time he didn't push it away. Now the tears came. They leaked down his cheeks as the idea took shape. Maybe there was only one way now. Maybe it had always been the only way.

The thought of it bored into the smallest places of

his mind and filled him with fear. He wasn't sure he'd be able to recover if he chose to walk the path in his mind's eye. Accepting defeat would be so much easier. But then he pictured his mother. He closed his eyes and searched for her soft voice, his heart in his throat.

You are the light of the world, my son.

He felt his resistance begin to soften. His mother had always told him he was light, and Zevonus had called him a light-bringer. He prayed they were right. Prayed he'd be able to walk into the valley of death and still remember who he was.

Below him, the terror had gripped the village. Groans of anguish filled the sky, a brutal reminder of the hell awaiting them if they disobeyed the Reds. Would he feel the same horror?

As the dread gave way to celebration, Jack sat in silence, alone with the choice that faced him. He blocked out the chanting and music and focused on the truth he knew in his heart.

He knew then that he would take that path, regardless of where it led him. He would take it because it was the only way to save his mother.

"For you, Mother, I will go into the darkness," he whispered into the night. His fear eased as her presence warmed him. "And I pray for the courage to find light in that darkness."

Jack swallowed. In the morning he would tell the Scalers of his decision. Tonight he would do his best to remember he was the light, and he would pray for the strength to remember in the days to come.

CHAPTER EIGHT

THE EARLY sun was just beginning to warm the sky when Jack made his way down from the treehouse. The rest of the Scaler village was stirring, making morning fires for breakfast, drawing clean water, and getting ready to begin their daily chores. Jack had spent the restless night tossing and turning, going back and forth, knowing what the morning would bring if he followed through with his decision.

"Stay!" one of the two guards stationed at the tree's base ordered.

Jack shook his head. "I need to speak to the Village Mother," he said. "She'll want to hear what I have to say, I promise you."

The guards exchanged a glance. "Then we will escort you."

"I'll meet her at the altar," he said. "Follow me if you

want. I'm not dangerous and I can't run as fast as you, so there's nothing for you to worry about."

He landed on the ground and glanced around the village.

"If you make any attempt to run or hurt anyone, you'll pay a dear price, boy," the guard snapped.

Jack dipped his head. "I know. Please tell the Village Mother and Camila that I have an announcement." He turned to the dragon altar and slowly walked forward.

One of the guards hurried past him, headed for the large cave. There's no turning back now, Jack thought. This is it.

There was no sign of Zeke's eye. Jack had already cried over the death of his friend, and though grief threatened to reclaim him, Jack pushed it down. He needed them all to know he was earnest, and crying over a dead Silver wouldn't help.

A quiver started in his fingers, and he balled them into fists to stop it. Reaching the altar, Jack took a final deep breath and climbed atop the small wooden platform. A chilly breeze swept past him as he locked eyes with the Scalers staring at him. More emerged from the large cave and tree huts. The guard who'd run to deliver his request to the Village Mother hurried into the cave. Jack wouldn't utter a sound until she was present.

Slowly, the gathering around the towering dragon idol swelled, as if sensing something important was about to happen. The pace of his heart increased with thoughts of what he was about to do. Still, he said nothing.

The guard emerged from the cave, followed by the Village Mother, Camila, and Sammie. More Scalers came out as the Village Mother and her entourage neared the altar.

Jack pressed his fingernails into his palms to still his shaking. He looked into Sammie's pale eyes looking up at him curiously. Then at Camila, who looked reserved but interested. He finally rested his eyes on the Village Mother. Her expression was controlled, her eyes calm.

"You wanted to speak with me?" she said in an even tone.

"Yes," Jack replied, then he glanced around at the Scalers. "I want to speak with all of you."

More than half the village was now present with others hurrying to see what the commotion was all about.

"So . . ." The Village Mother showed no sign of concern. "Speak."

Jack took a long, slow breath through his nose and let it out. "All of you know of me," he said, addressing them all. "I'm the boy from the stars with blood that's immune to dragon toxin. You all know I've refused to drink dragon milk, but I remain unaffected. I've befriended the Silvers."

The chirping morning birds were the only sound now. Every eye was fixed on him.

"Just yesterday I tried to use a Silver to turn Lukas." Jack searched the group and found Lukas scowling. "I thought if he could just see a different path, then he could be turned," Jack continued, eyes still on the dragon hunter. "I believed you were all deceived by the red dragons. That I was sent here to save you. To show you a different path on which you could be free from their lies."

The Village Mother was watching him carefully.

"But I know now that I was wrong," Jack said.

A few scattered whispers rippled through the crowd. The Village Mother's expression remained perfectly calm.

"I see now that the only way is your way," Jack continued. "I put my hope and faith in the Silvers, but I was a fool. I thought they could protect me, but seeing all of you—seeing the change in Sammie—I know that only the Reds can offer protection."

Jack let a moment of silence pass, thinking through his next words carefully. But Camila stepped forward and spoke first. "What are you saying?"

Here it was then. His fate was sealed.

"I'm ready to submit," Jack answered in a clear, strong voice. "I will drink your dragon milk and become a Scaler."

The group's soft whispers grew. He could feel both their excitement and hesitation.

"I knew he would see the truth," Sammie said above the whispers.

"He's a trickster!" Lukas cried. The dragon hunter stepped forward, eyes on him. "Why, after all you've done to undermine us, should we trust you now?"

His question silenced the crowd. They wanted to know as well. Jack had expected as much.

"I don't expect you to trust me right away," Jack replied. "I know I've made that impossible. But I'll show my loyalty. I will drink the dragon milk, participate in the ceremony, accept the terror and comfort, and you'll see that I mean what I say."

The Silvers had told him that only a redeemed Scaler could kill the dragon king. Until last night, he had not considered the possibility that the Scaler would be him. He would become a Scaler and pray that he would find redemption in time to kill the dragon king before his mother came to Earth in five days.

"I'm not sure that will be enough," the Village Mother said.

Jack looked at her, confused.

"You're the immune one. You've taken dragon milk and remained unaffected."

"I only drank a little," he objected. "And I was affected. I'm immune to their toxin, not their milk."

"Even so, never has a person tried so hard to destroy our way of life," the Village Mother snapped back. "Even with time, I will always wonder what your true intentions are."

She paused a moment. Then she pulled her mouth into a tight line and took a step forward. "I allowed you to come back because Sammie made such a compelling argument for you. Then you deceived my son, and for that I'm not sure I can ever trust you."

"I thought I was helping him," Jack said. "I was fooled by the Silvers and their message. I never intended to do anyone harm."

"I can't simply take you at your word. And I must protect my people."

Jack's mind scrambled. This wasn't working as he'd hoped.

"There must be a way for him to prove himself," Sammie said, daring to step toward the Village Mother. She's still fighting for me, Jack thought. Even in her blindness, she was his defender. "Some way to know his true intentions."

"It's not my place to read a person's heart," the

Village Mother said. "Only the queen herself can see through such deception. I'm sorry, dear Sammie, but there's no place for him here."

"Then take me to the queen!" Jack yelled.

The Village Mother turned back to Jack. Jack continued before she could speak.

"If the queen can see into my heart, then take me to her and let her decide my fate."

"Take you to the queen?" The Village Mother said, dismissal in her tone.

"It's perfect!" Sammie said. "The queen will know his true intention."

Camila faced her mother and spoke softly. "Would the queen not want to meet the boy with immune blood?"

The Village Mother considered the question, but it was Lukas who broke the silence.

"Send him to the queen!" he said. "If there's deception in his heart, the queen will destroy him."

"There is no deception in his heart!" Sammie snapped back. She looked up at Jack. "I know it."

Jack's heart seized. Would the queen be able to see his true motivation? Would she expose him and ensure the death of his mother? But he was already committed.

"Send him!" a Scaler Jack didn't know yelled from somewhere within the group.

Another followed suit. "Send him to the queen!"

"Yes, send him!" another cried out.

The Village Mother held up her hand to silence the crowd, eyes on Jack.

"You wish to see the queen?" she challenged. "Of your own free will?"

It was a strange question filled with warning, but he saw no alternative. "Yes," he said.

The Village Mother turned to Camila, who took a large drinking pouch from one of the guards. She handed it to the Village Mother, who held it up for all to see. Jack knew what it was without having to look.

Dragon milk.

His heart quickened.

"You may not enter the presence of the queen without first filling your gut with her milk," the Village Mother said. She approached Jack. "Drinking of her gifts will connect you to her. You've felt her presence before, but now allow yourself to feel her in a new way."

The Village Mother held up the pouch and Jack bent to retrieve it from her. He stood back up and uncapped the leather container. Any hesitation on his part would only undermine everything he'd said.

"Drink," the Village Mother ordered. "All of it."

Jack lifted the pouch to his mouth and swallowed. The sweet, warm milk drained down his throat, and a familiar hum edged into his mind. He could feel it seeping into his bones. Still he drank, draining the whole pouch.

He wiped his mouth with the back of his hand and tossed the emptied pouch onto the ground at the Village Mother's feet. "Take me to the queen," he said boldly.

The Village Mother gave a nod. "I will not be taking you." She tilted her head in a nod toward Sammie. "She will."

Jack turned to her, surprised. "You?" The effects of dragon milk began to take hold and for a moment he thought he might panic.

"I know the way," Sammie said, a dangerous glint of excitement in her eyes. "I've been there before." She stepped forward and held out a hand. "Come with me."

"Now?"

"The sooner the better. I'm sure she is eagerly awaiting our arrival."

He ignored the fear battering his mind and jumped to the ground. Sammie took his hand with a smile. She dipped her head at the Village Mother, then faced the villagers.

"I will take him to our queen so he can see her power and beauty like I have!" she cried. "And if I return alone, we will know he was deceiving us." She looked at Lukas. "But I won't be returning alone."

With that, Sammie led Jack into the thick woods.

She walked with some urgency, keeping her eyes forward, clicking softly, Jack's hand firmly in her own. Jack couldn't think of anything to say, and Sammie offered nothing. The dragon milk warmed his belly and flooded him with a strange brew of comfort and fear. He'd never had so much of it at once.

He was already beginning to forget why following the way of light and love was so important, and, realizing how quickly he was changing, he begged Yeshua to find him in the darkness that he was sure would swallow him. His mother depended on him. The whole world did.

Sammie led Jack through a row of trees onto a wide cliff ledge. Ahead of them rose tall, snow-capped mountains. Sammie gazed out at the sky, lifted her fingers to her mouth and let out a high-pitched whistle.

"Get ready for everything to change, boy from the stars," she said, throwing him a wink.

Almost immediately, the sound of heavy wings buffeting the air reached him, and he spun around to see two massive Reds emerging from the clouds, soaring directly for them. Jack swallowed deeply and stepped back as they approached, wide wings slowing their descent. Sammie stood firmly in place, wonder painted on her face. The ground shook when they landed and Jack took another step back.

He'd only been this close to a Red once before, when Sammie had been taken. Both Reds looked at Sammie as if for approval, then faced Jack. Black and haunting eyes stared down at him for a long, silent moment. Jack held his breath as one of them lowered its neck.

Sammie walked up to it.

Did she expect him to ride the Red? He'd ridden Silvers, but this . . . Even with the milk swimming through his veins, the thought terrified him.

Gripping the Red's scarlet scales, Sammie turned back. "Are you afraid, Jack?" she asked.

"Yes," he whispered.

"Good," she said. "Fear of the Reds is the beginning of wisdom."

Jack watched as she climbed up onto the first dragon. "Come," she said, perched on top. "They will take us to the queen."

On cue, the second dragon lowered its neck.

Without the milk, he would have run to the cover of the trees, but a part of him wanted to climb on the dragon's back and fly to meet his queen.

No, he thought. Not my queen. Rather, the queen who would die when he killed the king.

He clung to that thought as he struck forward on shaky legs, gripped the second dragon's scales, and hauled himself up onto its back. The smell coming from the Red reminded him of a strong acid, and he briefly wondered if the oils and sweat leaking from the Red would eat away at his skin.

Like fear. It eats away at us.

"Take us to the queen!" Sammie cried, face bright with excitement.

Jack had barely righted himself when the dragon under him leapt into the sky with a mighty flap of its glistening red wings. He lurched forward and threw his arms around the creature's neck so he wouldn't fall off.

Yeshua, protect me! I beg you!

Light filled his mind, then faded as the milk swallowed him once again.

Mother, please help me remember.

But Jack's memory kept failing him as the red dragons soared across the sky, taking him to their queen.

CHAPTER NINE

THE HIGHER the Reds flew, the colder the air became. Jack wished they would fly lower, like the Silvers had, knowing he would be cold up high. Sammie clung to her beast just ahead of him, so he couldn't see her face. And she didn't look back, making him wonder if she cared about him. She fixated on the tall peak of Mount Sneffels where the dragon lair awaited them.

Where the queen awaited them.

Thankfully, the cave entrance was below the snowy peak. They swooped down and settled on a narrow ledge in front of a large oval hole set into the mountain's jagged face. It was a good thing he hadn't tried to climb up here as originally planned. He wasn't sure any of the Dragon Slayers would have made it without falling. Like the Silver Towers, the queen's lair could be reached only from the air.

Unlike the Silvers' stunning home set like a jewel on the mountain, every bit of the scene before Jack was stark and dreary. The rock was gray, stained with dark blotches that might have been a fungus. The large oval hole entering the cliff looked like an empty eye socket that led straight to hell.

As the Silvers had said, the red dragons were fear itself, taken form. And in some ways, fear was hell. Jack knew this but was oddly torn between horror and the milk's comfort.

"You like it?" Sammie called, still perched on her Red.

Jack didn't know how to respond so he just looked at her.

She dismounted, slid down the Red's neck, and looked at the cave mouth. But she wasn't smiling anymore. "The fear will pass," she said. "Come on."

By the time Jack was on the ground, Sammie was already at the entrance, waiting. He walked on numb legs and then followed her into the cave.

The large tunnel was dark and smelled like mildew. Large torches on the walls cast an eerie light on the rock path. He doubted the dragons needed the light. They'd been lit for his benefit. Sammie could navigate the darkness using echolocation. Plus, she'd been here before. This truth had burrowed into Jack's mind, and he couldn't shake it. He may have given it more attention if the dragon milk wasn't consuming his brain.

They'd walked about a hundred paces when Jack made out a large archway ahead and faint firelight on the other side.

"What's that?" he asked.

Sammie walked on without responding. He followed her into a huge, domed chamber. A blazing fire at the center illuminated the room and five tunnels that led away from it. Dripping water echoed softly somewhere. Jack's fingers were trembling but he made no attempt to still them.

"I wanna show you something," Sammie said softly. She led Jack across the room to where a large square had been cut into the rocky wall between two tunnels. Jack paused and glanced down one of the tunnels as he passed it. More darkness. He shivered as a cool breeze from the shaft brushed his skin. He didn't want to know what was down there.

"Jack," Sammie said, waving him to join her. He walked to her side and copied her movements as she leaned over the window's ledge and looked down. Jack gasped at what he saw. Dozens of rocky ledges lined a massive cone hundreds of feet wide and so deep Jack couldn't see the base.

Every ledge was weighed down with dragons, some

lying, some crouched, others gnawing on trees and brush. Hundreds of them. Maybe thousands.

"The hive," Sammie whispered at his side. "Isn't it magnificent?"

He didn't speak. He couldn't. He just stared down in disbelief. The Silvers wouldn't stand a chance against such an army! A strange mix of horror and wonder washed through him. A part of him wanted to run back outside and scream for help, hoping the Silvers would save him. But the part of him swimming in dragon milk thought the hive was magnificent.

Were the Silvers really right?

Yes, he thought. But even that thought wasn't as strong as it had been before he drank the milk.

I'm falling, he thought. I can't stop myself.

"Come on," Sammie said, pushing back from the window. "We're nearly there."

Jack followed, trying his best to remember Yeshua through the fog of darkness that was drawing his mind deeper and deeper into itself. Moments of relief were quickly followed by more fear burrowing itself into his heart.

If remembering the light was hard now, how hard would it be after he became a Scaler? The question frightened him even more. But isn't that what Yeshua had done? The light of love had become human with all the fears known to humanity. His mother called it incarnation.

But Jack wasn't Yeshua. He was just a boy on a fool's errand. And his mother would have to become a Scaler to survive as well. Was that so bad?

He shook away the maddening questions and kept walking, following Sammie down one of the tunnels that led from the cavern with the fire.

They came to wooden double doors that towered thirty feet over Jack's head and were nearly as wide. On either side of the closed doors stood two Reds, eyes fixed forward, jaws firm and aimed directly ahead. Torches jutted from the walls, casting shadows that looked like boney fingers reaching for Jack's ankles.

Sammie came to a halt, and at the guard's command, the double doors slowly started to open. The wood creaked and the iron hinges squealed as the doors swung wide. Breathing heavily, Sammie stepped inside, eyes fixed forward.

Their steps echoed on the stone floor as they walked. At the far end of the torch-lit chamber sat a large throne of rock and iron. A throne for a queen, he thought. Not built like a chair but more like an altar, with rubies embedded in a black metal surface. A deep chill sank into Jack's bones. Jack could hear the soft breath of more dragons and saw half a dozen standing along the walls surrounding the throne.

Sammie held out her hand to stop him but he needed no encouragement. They stood side by side, both breathing heavily, both trembling.

The ground started to shake as a large beast emerged from the shadows at the back of the throne room.

Sammie, along with all of the Reds, knelt in response, but Jack was frozen in place as the creature came into the dim torchlight. The queen, Jack thought. She was the size of a Silver, so much larger than the other Reds, and draped in purple scales. Moving slowly, the queen slogged to the throne and perched upon it, royal purple scales glistening in the firelight.

The queen studied him through narrow yellow eyes. "Hello, Jack," she spoke to his mind in a soothing, soft tone. He wondered if Sammie could hear what he heard. Was the queen speaking to both of them at once?

"I have been waiting for you," the queen said. "And, yes, your friend can hear."

She shifted her eyes to where Sammie knelt. "Well done, my love. You have done as I asked, as you must do always and without hesitation."

"Of course, my queen," she said. "I will always serve when asked."

Without needing to be told, Jack's mind connected all the dots. This was why Sammie had insisted Jack could be trusted. She'd been entrusted with bringing him to the queen all along. No one was waiting for him to prove his loyalty, so he didn't need to play a role for them anymore.

Still on her knees, Sammie turned her head and glanced up at him. Her milky eyes shone in the dim room. Most of her expression was tainted by shadows, but even then, he could see that she was pleased with herself. Her obsession with dragon milk and her fear of the queen had drowned out her love for him. It had stolen their friendship and replaced it with fear. There in the darkness of the cave, standing before the queen, Jack felt a terrible sorrow for her. He would walk this path into the shadow of death for Sammie as much as for his mother.

"Still resistant," the queen said.

She had heard his thoughts. He was naked before her.

"You drank my milk. We are now connected and bound in my kingdom of fear."

There was no hiding here, so he spoke plainly.

"The Silvers told me who you really are," Jack said.

"I am power and safety," the queen hummed in his brain. "Did they tell you that?"

"They told me you are fear itself."

"Yes, fear that controls and protects. Tell me, what is wrong with that?"

Jack wasn't sure anymore, but he repeated what he'd been taught by his mother and the Silvers anyway. "Fear blinds the world to love," he said.

"You are wrong, little Jack. Fear is a form of love. I love them, so I protect them, and they fear that if they don't love me in return, they will all die an eternal death."

"But there is no fear in love," Jack said, again reciting his mother's words. "True love can't be threatened. It doesn't need to be protected."

A deep, rumbling laugh echoed through the throne chamber. It was different from the queen's tone—darker, drenched in power, sending a chill down Jack's spine. Long black drapes encrusted with fungus parted on the wall to Jack's right. He hadn't noticed it in the shadows. The low hum that often accompanied the dragon milk grew in his mind.

A monstrous dragon, larger than the queen by half, plodded into the light. The beast was covered in onyx-colored scales that reflected brilliant color across the floor. Its leather wings laid against its sides, and jaws large enough to eat a small house parted to reveal a mouth full of sharp, piercing white teeth.

The queen slid off the throne and moved aside as the new dragon took its rightful place. The dragon king.

Sammie whimpered. Still kneeling, her head tucked toward her kneecaps, her entire body quaked. Jack wanted to comfort her but was rooted in place. His own fear rammed like a bull into his heart.

The dragon king stood before the ruby-studded throne and turned his eyes to Jack. They were black circles rimmed in red. Other than the king, Jack was now the only one still standing—even the queen had knelt.

"Welcome to my kingdom," the dragon king said in a low, gravelly voice. Although his voice was speaking to Jack's mind, the king's words echoed audibly through the chamber. Jack hadn't encountered this kind of power before.

"Such a small power, and yet you are impressed," the king chided.

Terror silenced Jack. He wanted to say something but couldn't find his voice. The king's dark presence was crushing and intoxicating at once. This was the one who'd called for Dr. Alexander to kill him. Who'd turned Marco and Miguel into the worst versions of themselves. Who'd stolen Sammie's friendship.

"Come closer, boy," the king said.

Jack found his feet moving before he'd fully

decided to obey. Somewhere deep down, a small voice whispered through his mind: Remember who you are, Jack. But he wasn't able to obey that voice.

He stopped when he was close enough to feel the dragon's breath. It smelled like death.

"I've been waiting for this moment," the king said, his voice low, eyes locked on Jack. The dragon brought its head down and spoke softly as if for Jack alone.

"I want to show you what true fear tastes like," the dragon said. "It's the power that drives people to war. The power that must judge, because you can only judge what you fear. From that judgment comes condemnation and hatred. It's a power that once ruled religion and brought about the end of humanity. Would you like to taste that kind of power, Jack?"

He dared not hesitate. "Yes," Jack said.

Though you walk through the valley of death, fear no evil. The voice was hardly a whisper. He wondered if the dragon king could hear it.

"Good," the king said. It dipped its snout toward a tall, ornate gold chalice that stood at the base of the throne. "Drink from my cup and know true power."

Jack took a few steps to reach the gleaming gold cup. Three lines of onyx gems circled the top of the vessel. Thick gold covered the base. Inside, crimson liquid.

"Drink," the king said again.

Terror shook Jack's fingers as he bent and picked up the chalice. A strong putrid scent filled his nostrils and brought tears to his eyes. He stared down at the shimmering liquid as the small voice of peace continued to whisper in his soul.

Listen for my voice, Jack. I will be there in your darkest hour.

"Drink," the dragon king said yet again.

Jack lifted the chalice to his lips and drank. The liquid was warm and thick. It drained down his throat slowly and filled his gut. Darkness, thick and heavy, surrounded his mind and rushed across his flesh. Jack felt like he was falling into a deep pit. A black well that was swallowing him whole.

He fell until fear numbed his mind. Only then did he surrender to the darkness completely.

And in that deepest of fears, Jack saw; he saw that only the king could save him. Was saving him. Had saved him. Because fear, even though it was a lie, was his only true guide now.

"I finally see you, my son," he heard the king say.

My king, Jack thought. My father of lies.

"And how sweet are those lies," the king said. "Welcome home."

Jack opened his eyes and saw nothing had changed, except that he was kneeling on the ground before the king. That and his sight, which was now foggy. If his eyes had clouded, had his skin changed?

He lifted his arms and saw black scales matching the king's covering his flesh.

"Rise, my son," the king said.

Jack stood, sensing he was finally where he belonged.

"Receive my gift for you, my chosen warrior," the king said. He breathed into Jack's face, causing him to clamp his eyes shut. When he opened them again, he could see clearly.

"You will need your eyesight for what comes next," the king said.

Fear coursed through Jack. But his path was now the path of fear itself. It always had been. The light was only a figment of a deceived one's imagination. He was now the son of fear.

Jack bowed his head in total submission. "I will do whatever you ask, my lord," Jack whispered.

"Or die," the king responded. "What I say to you now will be heard by you alone. Do you understand?"

"Yes, my lord."

The king spoke his wish to Jack alone. The plan etched itself into his heart and mind. It was a terrible, powerful call for complete victory in the dragon king's name.

When the king was finished, Jack stood trembling, not daring to look up at his master.

"As you wish," he said to the king.

"Go, my son," the king said.

Without hesitation Jack returned to Sammie, who watched with wide eyes.

"Jack," she whispered, staring at his scales in amazement.

"Hurry," Jack snapped. "There is much to be done."

Any thought of who he was before was gone completely.

CHAPTER TEN

J ACK LED Sammie out of the dragon's domain to the high ledge where they first landed. The two Reds they'd ridden waited in obedience.

He stepped to the edge of the cliff and scanned the vast mountainous landscape spread out as far as he could see. To the east lay the Scaler village, wondering what the queen had decided, not knowing there was a king who ruled all queens. Far to the west hid the high mountain refuge of the Silvers. And above, far beyond the clouds, the Sanctuary. His mother.

He wasn't sure how he felt about it all. He was the son and servant of the king, and so of fear itself, the most powerful of all forces on Earth. Somewhere deep inside he knew his mother and the Silvers disagreed, but they were deceived.

His king had agreed he was the father of lies. That made Jack the son of lies. But those lies were now truth;

the only way to thrive on Earth was to embrace the reign of the Reds.

Terror flooded his chest, reminding him of the eternal suffering that awaited him if he slipped back into the Silvers' way ever again. The only way to find comfort was to embrace the reign of the Reds and obey fear. And obey he would.

"Jack?" Sammie had approached from behind.

He turned and walked past her. "Mount," he said, aware that he carried far more authority than he had only an hour earlier. This was the king's gift to him for the task that lay ahead.

Sammie hurried after him and they quickly mounted the two waiting Reds.

"Take us to the village," he ordered. The mighty dragons leapt into the air, flapping their massive wings to take them high.

Jack reviewed the plan the dragon king had given him alone. He felt the dark master with him in his mind, on his heart. The power he'd promised to show Jack pulsed like blood in his veins. His sight was clear and his mind was filled with darkness. Blackness, like his scales, shimmering in the sun.

Sammie had been right. The scales were beautiful. A sign of union. Armor given to him by his king. He would not fail. He could not.

Wind buffeted his face and hair as they flew high over the peaks. All he could see was his to control, not for himself, but for his king. All the while, fear was his constant companion, because only in fear could he ever find safety. That was the lie that was now true.

Right?

Terror seized him and he had his answer. But of course.

Jack saw the treetop huts come into view first, then the Scalers, who bustled about like tiny ants. The Red circled wide, letting out a thunderous shriek that drew the attention of the tiny villagers. The Scalers cried out in fear as they pointed and scurried to safety.

His dragon landed with a solid thump, followed by Sammie's. Jack slid down the Red's neck, landed on his feet and scanned the villagers watching the scene in awe. He whispered to the Red he'd ridden. With a dip of its massive head, the dragon returned to the air, followed by the second.

They would see each other again soon enough.

A stillness settled over the village, leaving Jack and Sammie standing in the center. The commotion had drawn the rest of the Scalers. All stared at his scales, a new and different shade than any had seen.

The Village Mother stepped through the crowd and slowly ran her eyes up and down Jack's new form.

"What is this?" she asked, sounding both intrigued and afraid.

"This is the mark of the king," Jack replied. He scanned the Scalers, who looked on in disbelief. "You must follow me," he cried out. "There is much to do."

Confusion broke out and the Village Mother slammed her grand staff onto the ground. Stillness settled over the village once again.

"You don't command my people!" she snapped.

Sammie stepped forward. "Actually, he does," she said. "He was blessed by the king."

"What king?" the Village Mother demanded. "We serve only the queen."

"Yes, and she serves the king," Sammie continued. "The dragon king."

Rumbles of surprise ran through the crowd. Jack watched, his mind fully on the plan. He didn't have time for this childish questioning, but he needed their help, so he would allow it for now.

"I saw him with my own eyes!" Sammie shouted. "I felt his power and watched the queen bow to him."

"Says the second child of the stars," someone blurted. "They are deceiving us!"

Sammie continued, unconcerned. "The king marked Jack as his own and called him son. You see now with your own eyes the king's scales bound to

Jack's body. Do you think we have the power to deceive you when the evidence of the king is so plainly before you? Watch your tongues if you wish to live."

Silence hung heavily over every soul. Even the birds quieted.

Sammie turned back to the Village Mother, whose shocked expression matched those of her tribe.

"Jack will lead us," Sammie said. "And you would be wise to follow." She returned to Jack's side, chin strong, eyes ready. "Who dares deny the king?"

Jack watched the Village Mother struggle to embrace such a dramatic turn of events.

"I will follow!" a familiar voice thundered.

Jack turned to see Lukas stepping forward, eyes certain. "The boy from the stars wears a mantle of power that cannot be denied. Any who do will surely face eternal suffering."

He dipped his head at Jack, who returned the gesture. Lukas was the beginning of the wave. One by one, a dozen more Scalers committed to follow.

The Village Mother approached and stopped four feet from Jack, eyes searching his. Slowly, she bowed her head, and when her eyes returned to his he knew they would all come.

"We will do as you command, son of the king," the Village Mother said.

Jack had never questioned whether he'd have their compliance—they were Scalers and would follow the way of fear. But standing there, surrounded by so many followers of fear, he couldn't deny the power of that fear. He had no ambition to rule them. He only wanted to do the will of the king.

He nodded at the Village Mother. "Very well. Follow me."

Without a glance back, Jack turned and headed toward a plateau the king had shown him in his mind's eye. Their task would begin there.

Without a moment's hesitation, the rest of the Scaler village hurried to catch up. They fell in behind, marching behind their commander, well over a hundred strong.

They walked steadily in silence for over an hour, perhaps fearing him. When they finally reached the plateau, the sun was already sinking. Evening would be upon them shortly.

Jack strode to the middle of the plateau where a large boulder jutted from the ground. He climbed up onto the rock and watched as the rest of the Scalers came to a halt, facing him. A warm wind whipped past his shoulders and ruffled the ends of his hair.

The dragon king had promised to be with Jack, and he could feel the beast now in the wind, in his body, in everything he could see. The presence filled Jack with strength and fear in equal measures.

"Brothers and sisters," Jack began. "Followers of the way of fear. For years you have faithfully followed the queen of Reds. In doing so, you have gained favor with the true source of your salvation. The dragon king."

None dared to speak as Jack continued.

"The dragon king drew me to Earth to lead you in your final struggle to be free. It is time to destroy all who stand against the king. You have been diligently hunted by the Silvers for many years. Now we will wipe them from the face of the Earth once and for all."

They stared up at him with wide eyes. Some inched closer, hungry for more, while others appeared to be genuinely frightened of such a prospect. Maybe they didn't believe it was possible.

"I see now that everything has worked out as the king has willed it." Jack looked at the Village Mother. "I've been with the Silvers in their towers. So you see, I know the way. And now we will destroy them there, where they hide from us all."

"This is true?" Lukas demanded. He pushed through the crowd before Jack could respond. "Then I will go! We must destroy them now!"

"You will," Jack replied, then addressed the entire crowd. "We will go as an army to the high point where they reside and end the scourge that has plagued Earth for so long."

"It is said that no man can approach their lair because it's too far and too dangerous," the Village Mother said. "How are we to take an army where not even one Scaler can go?"

Jack had expected someone would ask. He nodded at Sammie, who stood at his right like a lieutenant. As she'd done before, Sammie let out a high-pitched call into the air. For a moment nothing happened. Then Jack could hear them coming.

Distant at first, but growing every second, the clear sky began to fill with the rush of flapping wings. Jack didn't look up—he knew what was coming—but one by one the rest of the Scalers lifted their eyes to the sky. A gasp. Then more as they stepped back in awe.

Jack finally followed their stares and saw what they saw. A hundred dragons in perfect formation soared down through the clouds toward the plateau.

The Reds landed, one row at a time, shaking the ground. After the final row settled, fearful silence filled the air.

"We will ride on the backs of the Reds," Jack said loudly. "Their enemy is our enemy, and together we will cleanse the earth of anything that stands against us."

Jack faced the army of Reds and bowed his head

slightly. As one unit the dragons lowered their heads to the ground, showing their allegiance to the boy with the king's scales.

Jack turned back to the Scalers. "Tonight, we prepare for the war tomorrow brings. For the victory that will be ours. We ride at first light."

The dragon king whispered in Jack's mind. "Lead them to victory, my son."

Jack thrust his fist into the air. "For the terror and the comfort!"

The Scalers responded in kind, all with raised fists, voices loud and strong. "For the terror and the comfort!" Their words turned to war cries, the expectation of glory.

Jack turned his eyes to the Village Mother and saw her eyes bright with excitement. She bowed her head to Jack. Tomorrow they would destroy the Silver Temple and slay every Silver that opposed the king.

It was Jack's sole purpose.

The afternoon faded to evening and then night. The Reds remained on the plateau while the Scalers, led by Jack, returned to the village. They spent the night sharpening every spear they had and dipping the heads of each in Scaler blood, which was deadly to Silvers for reasons not yet clear to Jack. They painted their faces with black marks and dressed in leather armor more as a show of unified force than for the protection it offered.

Their protection was fear.

Jack spent most of the dark hours pacing the village, ensuring everything was ready. Scalers bowed to him when he passed by. He said few words, and even fewer were said to him. The entire village was focused on what the next morning would bring.

Jack finally retreated to a treetop hut where he stared at the stars, rehearsing the plan again and again. The door opened and Lukas stood in its frame, eyes on Jack, who turned back to the stars.

The older boy joined him and together they studied the skies in silence for several long minutes.

"Why has the dragon king never revealed himself before?" Lukas finally asked.

"I don't claim to know the ways of the king," Jack said.

"Yet you speak for him."

Jack searched the tall boy's face. "I do," he said.

Lukas looked down at the village. "I've never seen such a drastic transformation before."

"Is this a problem for you?" Jack asked.

"No, I'm just surprised by it." Lukas crossed his arms and leaned against the wall, offering a teasing grin. "I thought you were a Silver lover. I never thought I'd see the day you would lead us to slaughter them all."

A twinge of disgust filled Jack's belly. He was aware he'd loved the Silvers once, but the thought of them now made his stomach turn.

"I see everything differently now," Jack said. "I suppose fear changes the way we think."

Lukas nodded, studying Jack closely. "Good. Then we finally see eye to eye."

"Yes, we do."

"Then you have my spear," Lukas said. "Even to death."

Jack looked at Lukas and the two shared a silent moment. From enemies to brothers. They shared the same fear for what opposed the king and his law.

Nothing more was said between them, but Lukas walked at his left side as light dawned and one hundred Scaler warriors struck out for the waiting Reds on the plateau. The unified cadence of their boots on the ground reminded them all of their oneness in the great mission.

Each bore at least five spears. Each eagerly anticipated the coming victory. Each kept their eyes on Jack as he brought them to a halt on that plateau.

He faced them, Lukas and Sammie at his sides. "Mount now and trust the Red beneath you. They will follow me, not you. All you must do is remain in a state of humble obedience. Am I clear?"

"Yes!" they shouted as one.

"The time has come," he said, and walked to the same Red who'd delivered him to the village.

Although none of them had flown on Reds before, they dared not voice concern. If the children from the stars could ride, so could they. Within minutes all were perched atop their mounts.

"Take us where I lead," Jack said to his Red.

The dragon rose into the sky on powerful wings and, line by line, the others followed. A hundred dragons flew silently in perfect unison, eyes peeled for the first sign of danger. But there will be none, Jack thought. The Silvers were not creatures of battle. As Lukas said, it would be a slaughter.

Half an hour into their journey Jack held up his fist to bring the dragons into a holding pattern. Jack looked at Lukas, who flew close on his right.

"Circle here until I return. I'm going to the ship below us."

Lukas nodded, and Sammie called out from Jack's left. "Why are you going to our ship?"

"The dragon king asked me to deliver a message," Jack said simply.

"What message?" she pressed.

He hesitated. "A message for my mother."

CHAPTER ELEVEN

MICHELLE sat in the council room, her mind and heart buzzing with the communication they'd just received from Earth. Another Morse code message, but so different from the last one. Two days ago Jack had warned against coming to Earth, begging them to wait as long as possible so he could make the way safe. But this latest message reversed that warning.

Michelle replayed Jack's words over and over in her head as the other council members debated around the table. For my mother. The dragons don't need to be killed. I found another way. It is safe. Bring the Arc to these coordinates as soon as possible. Come to me, Mother. Earth is now our new home.

That was all except for the coordinates. Simple and brief, just like his other messages, but quite different in tone. She'd received four communications from Jack since he'd gone to Earth. All of them had included expressions of affection, which was Jack's natural way of being. This one was cold, distant. Or was she reading her own fears into the words?

Even so, he'd offered no explanation for why the dragons didn't need to be killed or what the other way was. Such a huge change of course surely deserved a few words of explanation, didn't it?

"Why are we still discussing this?" Lieutenant Rover said. "We should be preparing to leave."

"We've been preparing to leave for days," Rossa said. "Surely we are ready."

Captain Tillman gave a nod. "We're close."

"And then we take the Arc down?" Lieutenant Rover pushed.

Rather than answer, the captain looked at the council, inviting discussion.

"I want to point to this so we are all clear," Professor Dent said. "Living with dragons? Am I the only one who finds that insane? Are we sure the boy is still . . ." He eyed Michelle carefully. "In a stable state of mind?"

"That's the same song you sang when we first discovered dragons," Rossa pointed out. "The simple fact is, dragons not only exist but now live on Earth. If we hope to survive, we need to accept that and move on. My son gave his life to prepare a way. I suggest we take it."

Michelle spoke up. "Maybe. But I think Professor Dent's observation is worth noting." She was a woman of few words, but when she spoke they listened. "Not because I believe my son has gone insane, but because something about this does seem off."

"Off?" the captain asked. "How so?"

"I know my son well, and this message doesn't sound like him."

"It's Morse code, for heaven's sake!" Rossa snapped. "Not to discount your relationship with your son, but how could you possibly tell?"

She hesitated. "It's a feeling. Jack would know we would have this discussion, and he would've provided more information."

Lieutenant Rover frowned. "Well, there you go. Let's risk running out of air and suffocating based on the way Michelle feels about her son's message."

"Drop the mockery, Stephen," the captain snapped. "Everything we do is based on our interpretation of the evidence we have. Questioning that evidence is not only natural but critical to our survival."

The lieutenant sat back. "Forgive me. But we entrusted children to make Earth safe for our return. Our assumption was that killing the dragons would do that. But if eyes on the ground now say there's a better way, then who are we to disagree?"

The room was quiet.

The lieutenant continued. "Does anyone have a single piece of evidence that counters what the boy has said? Other than a feeling from his mother, or the professor's disdain for the thought of living in a world in which dragons exist?"

No response. His logic wasn't faulty.

"Or better yet," Lieutenant Rover carried on, "does anyone have another solution? Remaining here is out of the question. We're going to Earth whether we like it or not. So what's there to discuss?"

He was right, of course. There was no other way, at least none that Michelle could think of. They needed more time!

"You're right, Stephen," Michelle said, speaking in a gentle voice. She looked at the captain. "How much oxygen do we still have?"

"At our current reduced rate of consumption, ninety-six hours if we push it."

"That's four days," she said. "Why not send a message asking for more detail? If we hear nothing in three days, we leave."

"To what end?" Rossa countered.

"To the end that maybe, just maybe, something's happening down there that might change in the next three days. For all we know, someone other than Jack sent that message and we're headed straight into a trap."

"We don't have the luxury for maybes!" the lieutenant snapped. "What we know for certain is that without oxygen, we die a gruesome death. What we know is that we could land on Earth and remain in the Arc for some time before—"

"We're taking the Arc, not the whole space station, Stephen," the captain interrupted, pointing out the obvious. "Yes, we could live in the cramped quarters for maybe a few days, a week at most, but we still need food and water."

"So we either run out of oxygen here, or out of water and food on Earth," Stephen returned. "At least on Earth we would have access to far more information. My vote is with Jack. If he says he's found a way, we trust that he has."

"Assuming it was Jack who sent the message," the captain said.

"We have no evidence, other than a hunch, that it wasn't him."

Others began to chime in and Michelle could see the council would soon put the matter to a vote. Go to Earth now or wait. Majority would win. They would vote to go.

They did, with only Michelle and two others voting to wait three more days. Barring the discovery of new information, they would return to Earth within twenty-four hours.

Part of Michelle was as eager to go as the others. She longed to sweep Jack up in her arms. She longed to breathe Earth's air again, and plant a garden, and drink water from a stream, and laugh in fields of flowers with Jack.

But she couldn't shake the concern that gripped her heart as she made her way back to her pod. The moment the door slid closed behind her, she collapsed to her knees. The son she'd sent to Earth was lost. She knew it in her heart as only a mother could. It was in the words he used, the way he used them. It was in her suspicion that the dragons were not what they appeared to be. They weren't just beasts to live with, but something far worse. And Jack was lost in that world of dragons.

She couldn't share these thoughts with the others. Her suspicions were far too spiritual and lacked any evidence outside of a deep knowing. How could she speak to engineers and commanders about the forces of light and darkness at war in the hearts of all who lived? Her fellow council members had long ago cursed all religion.

There in her pod, Michelle's fears for her son swallowed her. She lowered her head and wept. She'd lost her husband, and now she feared she was losing her son. She knew this was his journey, and he'd been called to it, but the pain was too much to bear.

She hoped she was wrong. She hoped Jack really had found a way and they would be reunited in joy. But that hope refused to take hold. So she prayed for Jack and sent him love in whatever darkness he found himself in.

"See the narrow path, my son. See the only way and release your fear of it. Seek innocence in the face of judgment. Hear Yeshua's voice and see him in all you face. May love be your compass and may light be your shield." She sniffed as salty tears slipped past her lips. "And please, please stay safe, my dear, beautiful Jack. Your mother needs you."

CHAPTER TWELVE

THE ARMY of red dragons carrying one hundred heavily armed Scalers flew high through the early morning hours, sweeping west toward the Silver Temple. Jack rode his Red at point, leading the wide formation in silence. With each breath he was acutely aware of the dragon king's presence, watching, demanding obedience.

After sending the king's message to his mother, he'd considered her with some unease. He could see her face in his mind, knowing she would die in the Sanctuary if they ran out of oxygen. He couldn't seem to feel the same love for her that he'd once known, but he didn't want her to die any more than he wanted any Scaler to die. Summoning her and the rest to Earth so they could live as Scalers in service to the dragon king was the kindest thing he knew to do. They would all live under the rule of fear. Protected, alive, subservient.

They had flown for several hours when the Silver Temple finally came into view. They were there.

Sammie saw the towers as well and her eyes were bright. He gave her a nod and she whistled. Immediately, the formation shifted as planned.

Last night he'd gone over the plan of attack with his commanders—Sammie, Lukas, Camila, and the Village Mother. Each was assigned a group of twenty-five Scalers and a section of the towers: north, east, south, and west. He'd scratched a diagram into the dirt so they would know.

Jack knew a few things without question. One, the Silvers would never fight back. It simply wasn't in their nature, which was consumed with love, which they mistakenly believed would triumph over fear. Rather than fight, the Silvers would flee through the dozens of arched exits. Jack wasn't planning to spend his day chasing Silvers. Instead, he would post a red dragon carrying an armed Scaler at each exit. Once the Scalers secured the towers, the Silvers would be trapped. Truly, the towers would become their tomb.

Jack also knew that the tower walls acted as a barrier between those inside and the Reds. It was how the Silvers had remained hidden for so long. The dragon king couldn't communicate with any Scaler inside the towers. Neither could the queens of any of the Reds. For this reason, no Scaler was to set foot inside the towers.

Only he would go in.

The hundred Reds formed four V formations and descended fast on fixed wings, maintaining perfect silence. More details of the towers came into view. There were no Silvers posted at entrances or in the sky. No doves soaring about. The towers looked abandoned, and for a moment he wondered if they'd fled. But he doubted it. The Silvers were clever—they might even have anticipated the attack—but they were fools who placed their faith in surrender and love. Jack planned to use that weakness.

With an extended arm, Jack signaled the formations to attack. They soared past him with a mighty whoosh, then spread out to take their positions at each of the exits. He hung back, watching his plan unfold precisely.

It all happened quickly and without resistance. In less than a minute, every archway and exit was secured by at least one Red. The mountain towers were covered in a blanket of Reds like hornets on a hive.

Satisfied, Jack blazed for the main entry near the top of the towers. He felt surprisingly calm, comforted by the fact that he was in perfect obedience to his king. Nothing could hurt him as long as he aligned himself with the powerful beast that ruled this world.

The beast of fear itself.

His Red came in for a solid landing on the ledge in front of the main entrance. It took one step as momentum carried it forward, then came to a rest and folded its wings.

An eerie silence permeated the air. The main archway that led into the towers stood before him. Nothing else.

He slid off his dragon, three spears poisoned with Scaler blood secured across his back. Jack's feet hit the stone with a thud and he motioned for his dragon to stay put. The beast's dark eyes scanned for any threat.

Still not a sound from below. No shouts of victory or wails of death.

Jack took a deep breath and walked into the Silver Towers. The moment he crossed the threshold, the dragon king's dark presence lifted and he pulled up, disoriented. Like a vacuum, the towers seemed to have sucked him dry, leaving him feeling a void.

That void terrified him. All of the king's protection was gone here. He wasn't sure he could bear that! Dizzy with fear, Jack hurried back into the sun and there felt the reassuring presence once again.

The dragon king's comforting voice filled his mind. "Do not hesitate, my son."

He swallowed. "But I can't feel you with me."

"My fear is with you," his king said. "And you have my power. Your scales are proof."

Jack looked down at the beautiful shimmering scales that covered his skin.

"It is now your only purpose, my son. Do as I wish for the power I grant you."

Gathering himself, Jack walked back into the towers, mind fixed on the memory of his master. Once again, the king's presence vanished. Still, his heart was one with the king. Always.

Morning light streamed in through the beautiful stained-glass roof over the main sanctuary. He stopped. Many if not most of the Silvers were here, standing together, facing Jack, as if they had been waiting for him. Their eyes remained calm, blue and bright in the sunlight.

His eyes found Zevonus. The large Silver dotted with gold scales walked out and stopped twenty feet in front of him.

"Hello, Jack," Zevonus said. His voice didn't show a hint of fear. And it was curious that he could so easily hear the Silver. Maybe it would be harder outside, where the king's presence filled his mind.

"Zevonus," Jack said, dipping his head.

"You have returned," Zevonus said.

"Not the same me."

"So I can see." The Silver's calm annoyed Jack to his core. Didn't they know an army of Scalers waited to slaughter them all?

"Zeke is dead," Jack said, hoping to rattle him.

"His form was temporarily destroyed, yes, but Zeke is still with us."

A flush of rage spread across Jack's skin. These beasts were self-righteous fools. This planet would be better off when they were destroyed.

"You will all die as well," Jack said.

"So that is why you have come."

"You knew we would. You should have gone when you could."

"There's no place to go, young Jack," Zevonus said. "This is all part of love's path to redeem the fear that seeks to suppress it."

Love again. The word only deepened Jack's resolve to end the Silvers. "You're fools to think you could have won."

"There is no winning, and this does not end here."

"You're wrong."

"We shall see." With that Zevonus turned to the Silvers behind him. "You know what you must do."

Without hesitation or any hint of concern, they all turned and disappeared through the halls that led deeper into the mountain.

"Do you really believe you can hide from us?" Jack asked.

"Actually, we could," Zevonus said, turning back to Jack. "But you will see that we aren't. Do what you must, young Jack, but please do it quickly."

Jack held the old Silver's brilliant blue eyes for a moment longer than felt comfortable.

"Are you asking for mercy?" Jack asked.

"I'm asking you to do it quickly for your sake, not ours," Zevonus said.

Jack was taken aback. What was that supposed to mean?

"This is far from over, young Jack," Zevonus said. "And when you've finished doing what you feel so compelled to do, he will be waiting for you. Your mother will lead you to him."

Jack didn't know what Zevonus meant, but he knew his mother was attached to his old life, not the one given to him by the dragon king.

"Now I must leave you. I'll see you soon."

Zevonus turned and walked the same path the other Silvers had a moment earlier. Jack considered going after him, but a high-pitched whistle reached his ear. It was a Scaler signal coming from outside the towers.

Jack rushed back out the way he'd come. As soon as he entered the open air, the dragon king's heavy darkness smothered him, reassuring him once again of his path. He followed the sounds of ongoing whistles and distant voices laced with questions.

Jack scrambled up the Red's neck. "Take me up!"

The Red growled and leapt into the air, circling around so Jack could see the structure's face. Reds and Scalers covered every archway. Sammie was stationed on the west side. She stood in one of the arched exits, a Red at her back and a Silver before her.

As Jack watched from the sky, the Silver lowered its neck and placed its head at Sammie's feet. She jerked her spear back, angling the poisoned head at its exposed throat. Another whistle sounded from the east side and then the south. Jack ran his eyes across and saw more Silvers exiting the towers, then lowering their heads at the feet of the armed Scalers.

The warriors looked at one another, confused, surely wondering what kind of trick was being played on them. But Jack knew this was no trick. This was the foolish way of surrender the Silvers followed.

They were offering themselves to be slaughtered.

"Fools!" the dragon king's voice boomed in Jack's mind.

"Why would they do this?" Jack mumbled as much to himself as the king.

"Because they've abandoned common sense and wisdom. They believe nothing threatens them."

A distant note of familiarity whispered through Jack's mind, but he pushed it aside. It made no sense to lay down your life for your enemy.

The dragon king cooed in Jack's ear softly. "Now, my son. Kill them."

He hesitated. They were surrendering. There would be no victory in killing them now.

"Kill them!" the dragon king said again, this time his voice was low and cruel. "Kill them all! Do it for me!"

Of course, Jack thought. It was time to end this insanity.

He lifted his arm toward Sammie, who stared up at him from her platform. He brought his arm down swiftly, and with that signal, Sammie drove her spear into the Silver's neck. The beast at her feet moaned in pain as the spear's razor-sharp head sliced through his throat. Dark, red blood pooled under his head, and the Silver went still.

Filled with rage, Jack lifted both hands and

addressed all of the Scalers in one chilling command. "Kill them!" he screamed. "Kill them all!"

Groans of pain filled the air as each Silver died at the hands of a Scaler. Blood stained the stone platforms and ran over their ledges, marking their victory over the Silvers. No longer would they stand in the way of their master, king of all dragons, ruler of fear. Within minutes a spear jutted from the corpse of every Silver. It was finished.

Reds let out shrieks of pleasure and Scalers joined with cries of victory. They had come prepared for war but had slain their enemies without breaking a sweat. It was almost too easy, Jack thought.

He had to know their leader was dead. He flew back and forth across the face of the towers, searching for Zevonus. Twice, three times he circled and searched. There were many dead Silvers, but Zevonus wasn't among them.

Fear crept down his spine. The dragon king had called for the death of all, so Zevonus could not escape. He had to be absolutely certain.

On his orders, the Red he rode let out a thunderous roar, drawing the attention of all Reds and Scalers alike.

"Many have fallen at our hands today, but one is not among them," Jack shouted. "We will take the corpses of our enemy to present to the king. Prepare the dead. I'm going after their leader. Wait for my return."

Jack guided his Red high to the main entrance at the tower's peak. The dragon landed on the stone platform with a heavy thump.

Jack dismounted, removed a single spear from his back while casting the others aside, and stormed into the building. He would find Zevonus and slay the beast himself.

Then it would be finished.

CHAPTER THIRTEEN

J ACK STORMED into the towers, raging, but the moment he lost communication with the king, he slowed, unnerved. Heart hammering, he proceeded with more caution, carefully listening for any sounds that might lead him to his prey.

He followed the path he knew Zevonus had taken, a long, wide tunnel that turned often and descended sharply into the structure's guts. Where had the beast gone? Had he instructed the rest of the Silvers to lay their lives down to be slaughtered and then run to safety himself? He, more than the others, deserved to die.

It was dark. Without the sight his king had given him, he would have found himself completely lost. Even so, he began to wonder if Zevonus had intentionally misled him and escaped another way. Without the dragon king's presence, Jack felt vulnerable in the dark halls. It was amazing how quickly he'd become dependent on the king.

For what felt like an hour but surely couldn't have been more than ten minutes, Jack pressed on, confidence waning with each step. Finally, when he had all but given up hope of finding the Silver, the way ahead brightened. An exit?

Jack hurried forward and entered a large domed room. Daylight shot through a vertical shaft in the ceiling, revealing all, but there was nothing to be seen. The room was vacant, dusty from years of siting unused.

He peered up the shaft and was surprised to see that it rose only ten feet before meeting the blue sky. He'd been descending deeper into the towers, so how could there be open sky so close? Had he become confused and gone up rather than down? That was impossible.

A soft breeze swept into the room and with it a new sound to his right.

Jack.

His name, breathed on the wind. He whipped around but saw he was still alone. I'm hearing things, he thought. Or was this another tactic Zevonus was using to mess with his mind?

Jack.

This time his name was whispered from his left and he spun to see a tunnel that led deeper into the mountain. He was certain it hadn't been there only a moment ago.

Movement inside the shadows of the new tunnel caught his eye and he blinked. Two explanations streamed through his mind. One, he was in an unnatural space beyond ordinary reason, and his presence was already known by whoever had whispered his name.

Or, two, he was seeing and hearing things that weren't there. There was no tunnel and no one was calling his name. He decided this was the case.

He strode up to the tunnel and jabbed at it with his spear. The opening was real.

For a moment he just stood there, unsure of how to proceed. Then he remembered the king and his purpose here. Fear washed through his body at the thought of failing.

Calming himself, Jack walked into the tunnel.

Jack.

The call was louder this time, almost familiar. He pressed forward, walking faster. It had to be Zevonus, and Zevonus was powerless to harm him because love could not harm.

And why is that, Jack? he asked himself. Why does fear harm while love does not?

Something moved in the shadows ahead. Something much too small to be Zevonus. A form that looked . . . human—with their back turned to him, walking away down the tunnel.

Terror and curiosity raked Jack's skin. Maybe one of the Scalers had wandered into the towers despite Jack's orders.

"Who goes there?" he called.

His voice echoed but there was no response.

He followed and saw that the form was tall and thin, dressed in clothing Jack nearly recognized but couldn't quite place. It had long dark hair twisted into a single thick braid over the shoulder.

Jack.

Past his initial shock and hearing with a clearer mind, he realized the voice wasn't threatening. In fact, it was warm and comforting. Familiar even.

The stranger reached a junction and turned left, then walked out of sight.

"Wait!" Jack started to run, suddenly eager to know who it could be, thoughts of his mission momentarily lost. He reached the end, turned after the stranger, and pulled to a hard stop.

Jack stopped breathing. The stranger, a woman, stood in a small, well-lit room only ten paces away. She was bathed in a shaft of bright sunlight. Her kind eyes looked deeply into his soul, and her smile held his heart in a warm embrace.

It was his mother.

"There you are, my son," she said softly. He blinked, confused. Maybe she was only in his mind.

"I've been waiting for you here," she said.

But she hadn't been waiting here because she'd been leading him in the tunnel. Unless that too was his own mind leading him to her.

This had to be a trick. Zevonus's doing. A mind game to distract him while his prey escaped.

"You aren't real," Jack said, his voice flat and small.

She was looking at him with love and Jack found that love terrifying. He eased back, threatened.

"You aren't real!" he rasped.

She turned her head to a single wooden door that stood to her right. "He's waiting for you," she said.

"Who is?" Zevonus?

Her smile widened. "You already know the answer to that question. You've just forgotten."

He didn't know what she meant, but he hated the way she was looking at him. It made him feel . . . ashamed. He glanced down at his skin and was struck by how disgusting his scales were. He wanted to cover them so she wouldn't see. He wanted to run from the room so her eyes couldn't stare into his soul and see what was really there.

She slowly stepped toward him, a single tear

running down her cheek. "I am so proud of you, Jack. I love you with every fiber of my being."

Her words felt like a mallet slamming against his chest. If she knew what he was really like—what he had done and who he now served—she would be scolding him.

"You're wrong, beautiful boy. I love you as you are, right now. I always have and I always will." She faced the door again and he followed her stare. "And so does he."

He. Zevonus. It had to be. Jack was here to kill the Silver.

When he looked back to where his mother had stood, she was gone. He glanced around the room, but there was no sign of her. She'd just vanished.

He's waiting for you.

Her voice drifted to him on another faint breeze, but she was nowhere to be seen.

Jack turned back to the single wooden door. It was a trap. He should leave this place. But he couldn't make his feet run away, because he'd come to kill Zevonus. If he failed, he would suffer at his master's hand. He had to see what lay beyond the door.

Heart in his throat, Jack crossed to the door, put his hand on the single iron handle, and pulled it open. Light blinded him and he raised his hand to protect his eyes. A cool breeze brushed his skin, carrying the scent of flowers. Birds chirped and he knew he was outside.

When he lowered his hand, he saw that he was standing in a stone courtyard under a bright sun. He wasn't deep in the towers, but at the very top. But how could that be?

If he were outside he could reconnect with the dragon king, to find the comfort and safety he desperately needed.

"The king cannot see you while I am here," a calm voice said to Jack's left.

He twisted to see a man with olive skin and bright blue eyes sitting casually on a stone bench. Eyes like the Silvers'. He was wearing a simple tunic, his hair short and well kept, his smile bright and easy. Jack couldn't remember ever seeing him before, but something about him felt familiar.

"You know the king?" Jack asked.

"Of course," the man said. "And I know you too, Jack."

He did? How? "But I don't know you."

"This face I wear may look unfamiliar, but I've always been with you, my dear friend."

The fear inside Jack roared like an outraged lion crouching before a hunter. Jack inched back, hands gripping his spear. "Who are you?" he stammered.

"People call me many things," the man said. He leaned forward so his elbows were resting on his knees. "You can call me Yeshua."

The name cut across Jack's heart and the darkness in his mind screamed.

The man who called himself Yeshua held Jack's eyes with a warm intensity that immobilized him. He wanted to run. To flee this place and find himself in the comforting arms of his master, the king of dragons.

Instead, he just stood there, trembling as tears gathered in his eyes, confused by his reaction to the man.

"You're confused because fear blinds you and shows you darkness rather than light," the man said. "And so you stumble in darkness."

"The whole world is darkness!" Jack blurted. "Every turn brings more threats and harm. Everyone I've ever loved will die without the protection of fear!"

"And what exactly do you need protection from?" Yeshua asked, brow raised.

Jack swallowed. "I already said. Threats of harm. Of the enemy."

The man tilted his head. "That's what you're afraid of? An enemy? The only enemy you have is fear itself, which is a lie. I should know. I once lived in a body and overcame the world of fear through my death and

144

resurrection. I made a way for you to see as I see as you follow that same path. In love, there is no fear, and so no enemy—at least not one that can threaten you. Anything you think threatens you is only your own misperception because of your blindness to love—to God—the source of your being who is love."

Seeing through the terror in his mind, Jack recalled his mother sitting beside him as a small boy. He'd locked the memory away in his heart. She read the ancient teachings of Yeshua to him. Her laughter was warm, her voice sincere. Jack had beamed up at her as if she hung the moon and stars outside their living pod window.

More tears filled his eyes, and the fear inside him snuffed out the memory.

Yeshua leaned back on the stone bench and nodded at the spot beside him. "Come and sit with me, Jack. Let me tell you who you really are beyond your fear of not being enough."

Fear rooted his feet in place. He couldn't disobey the dragon king. But his soul yearned for the love he could feel from this man. A love he had once experienced but could now hardly grasp. Maybe he'd never really experienced it at all. Not the kind of love that knew no fear.

"You cannot serve two masters," Yeshua said,

reading his heart. "You can serve fear and continue to see the world as the terrifying place you think it is. Or you can come sit with me and let me remind you of a love in which there is no fear. The world looks very different through the eyes of true love."

Jack swallowed as a tear dripped from his chin.

"Only you can decide, Jack," Yeshua continued. "But I tell you this. My love for you will never waver, because love holds no record of wrong, even for a moment. It can't be threatened, because it's infinite. Regardless of how you see the world and yourself, I will always see you as beautiful, shameless, and full of light, even if you are blind to it. Those are the names I gave you. They are your true identity. You are simply lost. And in that darkness you serve fear and offer more fear to the world. Indeed, the whole world is lost in the darkness of fear."

Like an icepick chipping away a frozen crust, the man's words began to break the encasing of fear around Jack's heart.

"Come and sit with me, Jack," Yeshua said.

Jack trembled as shame washed through him again. "But I'm covered in scales. I can't sit by you like this."

"What scales? I only see you," Yeshua said.

Jack lifted his right arm to show the scales and

gasped. There were no scales! His skin was clean, pure. The dragon king would be furious! Jack looked back at Yeshua, mouth open in disbelief.

"What did you do to me?"

"It's how I see you in the love that holds no record of wrong. No scales or scares or imperfections. I don't bind you to those things; only you do that." Yeshua patted the empty place on the bench playfully. "Come. This seat has your name written on it."

Fear told Jack he would surely pay for this. There would be a reckoning with the dragon king and soon, but he was so drawn by Yeshua's presence that Jack finally crossed the platform and sat next to him.

"Good." Yeshua patted his knee. "The first thing you must realize is that unless you become like an infant once again, you won't be able to see the kingdom of heaven that's already here, in your very being. It's like being born all over again. To see that kingdom is to see light and love where you once saw darkness and fear. You've heard this, yes?" Yeshua said.

Jack nodded. His mother had read it to him from the ancient text.

"Do you know why this is true? Because little children haven't yet learned to see the world through the eyes of fear. They see the world without judgment.

Yes, they cry when they're hungry, but they see both the cockroach and the butterfly as wonders to behold. Isn't that right?"

Jack's chest felt tight, making it hard for him to breathe. Part of him was resisting what he heard, but another part of him was desperate to know such a love and see that light.

"Yes," he said.

"Yes." Yeshua chuckled. "The only real question now is, will you say yes to seeing the kingdom that I see instead of the kingdom of darkness that fear shows you?"

Jack sat still, daring not to speak, because to say yes meant to deny the king of dragons.

"It's your choice, my dear friend. Yours alone. Say yes to fear or say yes to the love I will show you." Yeshua turned his shimmering blue eyes to Jack. "What will you choose?"

"I . . ." Fear was trying to pull him deeper, but he was seated in the light of Yeshua. There was hardly a decision to be made, he realized. He had to see the light! He so desperately wanted to know Yeshua's love that could see no threat. Not even a threat from the dragon king.

"I want to see the kingdom of light," he said, and the moment he did he was desperate for more. His fear eased and tears spilled down his cheeks. "Yes," he croaked, staring up at Yeshua. "Yes, I will say yes to you and your love."

Yeshua dipped his head once, bright blue eyes gleaming with delight. "Perfect. Your sight of the kingdom will blossom as you follow me in the way of that love. As I once said, the one who practices the truth comes into the light. And that truth is always a love that holds no record of wrong." He winked. "But maybe you would like to see what I see now."

Jack nodded because he couldn't speak past the lump in his throat.

Yeshua placed a hand on Jack's knee. The world immediately shifted. Like darkness vanishing in the light, all the fear in Jack's mind and heart was no more.

And in that moment, he saw only light and beauty and love. The birds' calls sounded like a chorus of angels in the heavens, and the air felt like the breath of God. But more, he saw that he was the son of the Father, being reborn with the sight of an innocent child. This is what it was like to see the kingdom of heaven while on Earth!

The stark shift from darkness and fear to light and love was so drastic that his bones began to tremble.

Jack closed his eyes as his mother's words poured through him—the words she'd read in that ancient, forbidden text. Like Yeshua, he was also the light of the world. He belonged to love, a love in which there was no fear. An unconditional love that fear hated because in such a powerful love, fear itself had no power. It didn't exist there. He wasn't even sure the dragon king really existed, at least not here in this kingdom.

Tears now gone, Jack chuckled as the warmth of Yeshua's love, which was now his own, swept through him. He felt an arm around his shoulders, pulling him close.

"Keep your eyes closed, Jack," Yeshua said softly. "Now, look out at the world in your mind's eye and tell me what you see."

He'd played this game with his mother a hundred times. In his mind's eye, he could see light outlining everything. The mountains, the trees, the fields, the clouds. There was nothing to fear, nothing to judge, nothing but beauty and love swimming in full color wherever he looked. This was the world before the knowledge of good and evil had blinded it.

But Yeshua had come to bring sight to the blind. And, as his mother said, God was everywhere at once. Omnipresent, she called it. So that light must also be everywhere at once. That's what he was seeing.

"It's how I see the world," Yeshua said. "With eyes

of innocence, like a little child. You too can be in this world of fear without being bound to it. In it but not of it. The blind will lead the blind, but you, Jack, can see the light in the darkness and lead others to that light."

Jack opened his eyes and looked up at Yeshua's kind face.

"That's why I called you here," Yeshua said softly. "Because you, more easily than most, can see with my eyes of innocence and love as your mother taught you. They don't see love, Jack. They see darkness instead of light. They've forgotten me and covered up the light."

Jack felt another wave of emotion gathering in his throat. "I forgot you, too," he whispered.

"And yet you are forgiven," Yeshua said.

"What if I forget again?"

"There is no limit to forgiveness," Yeshua said, eyeing him kindly. "Do you love me, Jack?"

"Yes."

"Then show them my love."

"What if I can't?"

Yeshua smiled. "Do you love me?"

Jack nodded.

"Show them my love."

"I just don't want to let you down," Jack whispered.

Yeshua held his eyes. "Do you love me?"

"You asked me that three times," Jack said. "Don't you believe me?"

"Of course I do," Yeshua said. "The better question is, do you believe?"

Jack thought about his words. He thought maybe he was beginning to understand what everyone had been telling him. His mother, Zevonus, now Yeshua. It was Jack's choice to serve Yeshua or the king of dragons. To see the world in love or fear. Jack knew about love—his mother had made sure of that—but had he ever fully believed it? Had he ever fully stood in love beyond any fear?

"Good," Yeshua said softly. "When the time comes, remember that those who enter my kingdom do so in great force, as written. But that force is the light of love used against fear and nothing else. Not against those who live in fear, or the Earth, or anything else, but against fear itself. Know that, my young friend. So few have."

Jack nodded. "I will."

He looked out across the landscape. It was beautiful but what anyone would expect to see: mountains with sharp edges, grassy fields, tall trees, colorful leaves. With a deep breath Jack changed his perspective and looked again. The world shifted, and brilliant colors glowed from every inch of the scene before him. Love.

"Ah yes," Yeshua said with a soft chuckle. "Now you can see."

"Yes," Jack said. "Now I can see."

CHAPTER FOURTEEN

TIME SEEMED to stand still while Jack sat on that stone bench, basking in the love of Yeshua. All the pressures and troubles that had felt so important throughout the course of his life suddenly seemed so small. The longer he sat there wrapped in perfect love, the more he knew that this was the way life should be. It was like a return to the garden of Eden his mother had told him about. Life lived through the eyes of Yeshua in which there was no darkness or fear. It didn't even exist as he looked across the plain.

He was seeing the kingdom of heaven.

But Jack also knew he could easily return to the old way of seeing through the lens of darkness. In that place, fear would return like a crushing wave. Forgetting Yeshua's love was really the only problem that ever threatened the earth.

"It is time, Jack," Yeshua finally said.

Jack shook his head. "I don't want to leave you."

Yeshua chuckled. "You don't have to. I am with you always, even when you see darkness instead of light."

Jack thought through the task ahead. He felt so different. He could see the trouble, but he wasn't afraid. How could he when he was wrapped in the warmth of Yeshua? It was like a superpower.

"The dragon king will know that I don't serve him anymore," Jack said, not afraid but aware.

"He will sense a disturbance, but I will block him from seeing your heart," Yeshua said. "And I will give you back his scales."

"But I will still be in your light," Jack said.

"Of course."

A shadow briefly crossed Jack's mind. What about all the Silvers they'd killed? How was he supposed to kill the dragon king? Would his mother return and die from the dragon toxin? Was he strong enough?

His path would lead him back into the darkness. Back into ideas about who he was and what he was capable of and what the world was—ideas that were Jack's and not Yeshua's. Ideas created in fear and not in love. Would he be strong enough to overcome the darkness he would surely encounter?

"There is one more thing you should know, young

Jack," Yeshua said. "The dragons live in your mind. They have no power beyond that which you give them."

Jack blinked. "They're not real?"

Yeshua chuckled. "Oh yes, very real. But only because you empower them through fear of them. You will see that. The Red dragons are fear made into form. The Silvers are the spirit of love made into form as well. But truly, both are in your heart as you choose to surrender to one or the other. Remember that when the darkness comes to pull you back."

Jack nodded, emboldened by the light. "I will," he said. He looked up into Yeshua's blue eyes and felt the man's love flowing through him. "I think I'm ready."

Jack stood with Yeshua, who wrapped him up in his arms and placed a soft kiss on the top of his head. "Go in my love, my young friend."

"I will," Jack said. He left the room the same way he'd entered.

The moment the wooden door closed behind him, Jack wanted to be back on the bench with Yeshua. For several seconds he stood outside the door and replayed the amazing encounter. Then, unable to stop himself, Jack turned and reopened the door to see Yeshua one more time.

The room was empty. Bench and man gone. Jack had almost expected that. Had it all been in his mind?

It didn't cause fear or discouragement. It didn't matter whether the encounter had happened in real time or in his mind. He was changed either way. He might not be able to see Yeshua's form, but he could feel him everywhere.

"Hello, Jack," a warm voice said.

Startled, Jack spun around, surprised by what his eyes saw.

"Zevonus," he whispered. Struck with deep emotion, Jack rushed across the room and wrapped his arms tightly around one of the Silver's legs.

Zevonus didn't flinch or resist. "It is good to see you have returned, young Jack," the dragon chuckled.

Jack pulled back. "We killed all the others." He felt sadness but no shame. There was no shame in love, and he was still swimming in that love that held no record of wrong.

"You did. But not really. Unlike the Reds, we Silvers cannot die."

It made perfect sense to Jack.

"There is something I want to know," Jack said. "Why does Scaler blood on a spear kill a Silver?"

"Because Scaler blood is tainted with the Reds' milk. It is filled with blindness and deception, which effectively kills a person's relationship with love. In using their blood to attack a Silver, the Scalers finally sever the last of love in their own hearts."

It made perfect sense. As Yeshua had said, the dragons lived in their minds.

"But love is never dead," Jack said. "It only becomes unseen."

"Now you know."

"And now I'm the redeemed Scaler who gets to kill the dragon king," Jack said. "But how?"

"Do you still have the gift I gave to you?" Zevonus asked.

Jack had completely forgotten. He dug his hand into the collar of his shirt and yanked out the small chain. The silver ring dangled from it.

"When the time comes," Zevonus said, "wearing it will give you the power you need. You will see."

"Until then, I'll keep it hidden. I don't want the dragon king to see it," Jack said, tucking it back under his shirt.

"There is a large silver bowl close to the outer door," Zevonus said. "I have put Silver blood in it for you. Dip your spear in it before you leave so they believe you've put me to rest."

"You knew I was coming for you?"

"But of course." He winked.

Jack grinned.

"Remember, young Jack, whatever you place in darkness calls you to that darkness, which is fear. And fear always calls more fear to itself. Only love turns fear into shadows. The ring on your neck will show you that when the time comes."

Jack nodded. "Okay."

"Now go and do what you have chosen to do." Zevonus dipped his head toward one of the tunnels leading from the room. "That way will lead you back to the others. I will see you soon, my friend."

Jack gave Zevonus's leg another hug and then followed the tunnel to the main sanctuary near the top of the towers. As Zevonus had suggested, he dipped his spear in the bowl of Silver blood near the entrance. Filled with love but disguised in the dragon king's black scales, he headed into the bright sunlight.

The moment his red dragon saw him, it let out a shriek to announce his return. With that shriek, the dragon king's dark presence swarmed Jack. He was back in communication with the beast, and the full brunt of that darkness nearly took his breath away. He felt a compulsion to rush back into the towers.

Instead, he walked out for all to see him, hefting the bloody spear high.

"Is it done?" the dragon king's voice hissed in Jack's mind.

"It is finished," Jack replied. And it wasn't a lie. It was finished, just not in the way the dragon king expected.

He could feel the king's pleasure, and it made his stomach turn. But the king apparently hadn't picked up on any change in him. Blinding the king was Yeshua's gift to him for the task at hand.

"Take them to the village and burn their bodies," the king gloated. "All will see the Silvers dead."

"As you wish," Jack said.

"Tomorrow you will bring the others to me. All of them."

"Where?" Jack asked.

"To the valley of death," the king growled. "There, I will make them all my people."

Jack hesitated. "How will I find it?"

"The Reds will know."

"As you wish."

Jack mounted his Red, and it lifted into the warm midday sun, circling back so he could be seen by all. As instructed, they'd strung the bodies of the Silvers to the Reds using long ropes and waited for him.

Jack thrust his bloodied spear into the air and cried out at the top of his lungs, "Their king is dead!"

He scanned the army as his dragon held space, feeling the presence of the king deep in his bones. But more, he saw the light. Everywhere he looked, he could see Yeshua's light. It took his breath away.

"Brothers and sisters," Jack cried out. "Today we slew our enemy in full. In service to our king we have won. It is finished!" He thrust his spear into the air so the others could see the blood of a Silver drip down from its tip.

A hundred Scalers roared their approval. The valley filled with the shrieks of red dragons. Jack held the spear high for a moment and let his blind brothers and sisters rejoice in what they had done. They had come to conquer and they had. But love had not been defeated today. Indeed, it had gained more ground than any would dare imagine.

Satisfied, the Scalers quieted and looked up at Jack, waiting for his command.

"We go home!" he cried, and swept his dragon toward the east.

Hours of flying passed by in a fog. Reds all around, Scalers riding upon their backs, dead Silvers suspended beneath them. There were forty-seven Silvers in total, each bound in thick ropes hanging between two Reds, trophies of the Scalers' war.

Jack kept his eyes forward. There is no fear in love,

he reminded himself over and over. Lead them now to free them later.

The village came into view and Jack led the Scaler army down. Those who'd remained rushed out to greet the large formation.

In groups, the Reds landed, released their riders and the Silvers, then took flight, headed west. Children danced at the sight of the dead. Cries of victory and joy filled the village. There could be no doubt now.

Their great enemy, the Silvers, were all dead.

"Well done, my son," the dragon king whispered.

Jack bowed his head silently in response. The king would be watching. This wasn't over yet.

A heavy hand came down on Jack's shoulder. He turned to see Lukas smiling. He gave Jack's shoulder a squeeze and let out a loud laugh. "We are victorious, my friend!"

"Yes," Jack replied with a smile. "You all did well."

Lukas pulled something from his side pouch and held it out toward Jack. It was a dagger, a wooden handle with an eight-inch silver blade that had something inscribed on it.

"My mother gave this to me," Lukas said. "It belonged to my grandfather. The words are Latin: Veri honoris. 'For truth and honor.' I want you to have it."

Jack looked from the small blade back to Lukas, uncertain.

"You brought my people out from the constant shadow of our enemy," Lukas said. "Something I couldn't have done. It should be yours."

Jack knew better than to refuse the gift, so he took the dagger from Lukas. "Thank you."

"Now," Lukas said, giving Jack's shoulder a playful punch. "We will celebrate all night! Come."

It was the last thing Jack had any intention of doing.

"You should celebrate," he said. "And you are to burn the bodies of all the Silvers. But I won't be attending. The king has more for me."

Lukas gave Jack a proud nod. "And we will all follow you, son of the king."

Even now, Jack could see the light of Yeshua trying to break through the scales that covered Lukas's heart. He gave Lukas a nod, and the older boy turned back to the others caught up in their defeat of the Silvers. If only they knew what they were celebrating.

Jack turned from the village, tucked the blade into his belt, and left them to their deception.

Tomorrow they would all see the king in the valley of death.

CHAPTER FIFTEEN

JACK WOKE early and watched the sun rise from the hill south of the village. There was nothing new to learn now, only a place to be, and that place was in alignment with Yeshua's light. That light was also his own now, expressing in darkness as the love that knew no fear. That light of love would obliterate the darkness of fear. His role was simply to kill the prince of fear, which was the king of dragons.

If he had an enemy, it wasn't the Scalers or any other thing on Earth. It was fear itself, which had manifested in form as the red dragons, their queens, and the king of all dragons. Killing the dragon king was an act of love, because the dragon was fear and only perfect love, Yeshua's unconditional love, could cast out fear.

He felt no fear as he sat on the hill and trained his mind on the light, but he knew he would in time. As

Yeshua had said, his sight of the kingdom was still blossoming. So he surrendered himself and clung to trust. Really, it wouldn't be him killing the dragon but Yeshua's love and light, expressed through him.

This much was clear to him. Less clear was how it could be done.

The sun had just crested the mountain when he woke Lukas, who was still slumbering after the late night of celebration. There were surprisingly few ashes in the huge firepit where they'd burned the Silvers. No bones, no charred flesh, only charred bits of wood. It was as if the Silvers' remains had vanished.

"Where are we going?" Lukas asked, rubbing the sleep from his eyes.

"To the Valley of Death," Jack said.

The Village Mother approached from the cave. "The Valley of Death?" she asked with some concern. "I've never heard of it. For what purpose?"

"The Reds know where it is. The king calls us all to meet them on the plateau."

"All?"

"Every man, woman, and child. We leave in thirty minutes."

With that, he made his way to the village outskirts and waited. The village was soon a hub of activity. They all stumbled into the light and rushed about preparing the children and the aged for what promised to be a day to remember.

When they'd gathered, he led them to the high plateau as he had before. Once again, the Reds were waiting for them, more than a hundred to accommodate both lone riders and families.

Once again the Reds lowered their heads to be mounted. Once more they took flight and quickly formed a wide formation that darkened the sky. But this time they flew east, where few Scalers ever dared venture.

East, toward the Valley of Death.

The flight only took thirty minutes. All the while, Jack tried to rest in the truth Yeshua had given him, but as the mountains yielded to a deep valley far ahead, fear began to crawl through his skin. Even from this distance he couldn't mistake the red dragons perched along the rim of the cliffs that ran the length of the valley. Thousands of them, far too many to count.

He glanced to his right where Sammie flew, staring ahead. Lukas flew to his left, mouth agape. Both were fixated on the sight.

Jack surveyed the landscape as their Reds made a sweeping descent. The Valley of Death is more a canyon than a valley, he thought. Tall red cliffs bordered the narrow valley, and the barren ground between them was empty and cracked. The only way in or out appeared to be from the sky or from the south, but it would be a very long hike on foot.

Jack saw the dragon king on a massive stone platform at the north end, and his breath caught in his throat. His black scales shimmered against the red cliffs. Behind him stood two queens, purple scales shining like jewels in the sun. Regal. Intimidating. But nothing compared to the king, who strode back and forth in wait.

Their Reds swept down and landed on the parched earth before the king. The Scalers remained atop the Reds as silence filled the canyon. For a few moments Jack sat still, eyes fixed on the king, whose dark, narrow eyes bore into him.

"Well done, my good and faithful son," the king said.

Jack dipped his head, and immediately the dragons they'd flown on lowered their heads so the Scalers could dismount. They dared not utter a word, hushing their children, many of whom began to cry in the presence of so much fear.

Their Reds remained on the canyon floor as at least a thousand Reds from the cliffs leapt from their perches and glided down to fill the barren earth behind them.

They were in an arena of sorts, surrounded by a writhing sea of Reds. Silenced children gripped their mothers' legs, most trembling at the sight of the black king and his many servants.

Jack stood at the front, eyes fixed on the black, soulless eyes of the beast he had come to kill. Yeshua had said the dragons were in their minds as well as in form, and he didn't know how that could be, but he clung to the knowledge now. He was facing his own fear. They all were. Only the light could dispel this darkness deep within them all.

A deep compulsion to kneel before the king swept through him, and, although he was loath to do so, he had to maintain the charade. He had no plan, no thought of what he should say or do—only a simple faith that if he set his intentions on the light, all would be made known here in this Valley of Death.

Jack slowly settled to one knee and the rest of the Scalers followed suit.

Satisfied, the king spoke to their minds without moving his mouth.

"Welcome, my children," the king said. His guttural voice was low and clear. "I have waited so long for this day. For years I have watched you serve my queens. For years I have watched you faithfully drink their milk and follow the law. For years I have watched you tremble in fear and celebrate the comfort I offer as you worship me, your king. And I am pleased."

Deadly silence hung over them all. If the Reds behind Jack were breathing, Jack couldn't hear them. There was only the sound of the king's voice and the steady thumping of his own heart.

"You have been faithful, understanding the wisdom of fear. For who is one without fear? Fear is what keeps us safe from the hells of this world. Without fear, we are vulnerable and naked. Without fear, we face eternal suffering."

Yeshua's words echoed in Jack's mind softly like the whisper of the wind.

Fear is a lie. The father of lies.

Warmth touched the edges of his heart. The message of the dragon king was clear. Without fear, you cannot be protected from the troubles of the world. From death. But the message of Yeshua was also clear. In love, you cannot be threatened by the troubles of the world. In love, death has no sting, because Yeshua has already overcome death.

It had never been so clear to Jack as it was now. He could not serve two masters. Either he would live in fear, or he would live in love. A love in which there was no fear.

Could it really be that simple?

"Today," the dragon king continued, voice rising, "I have found each of you worthy. Because you have obeyed my law and slayed the Silvers, who stood against me"—the king spread his wings and lifted his head to the sky, roaring his final words—"I will make you as I am, in my kingdom."

The ground shook as thousands of Reds roared their approval, jaws wide.

The Scalers trembled. Children screamed. But Jack knelt in silence as clarity filled his mind.

Fear had created a false hope for a kingdom of comfort and peace. But it was all a lie! The true kingdom of peace was already here, available to all who surrendered to the light and love. All here had been created in the perfect image of that love. Created in the image of God, who was love.

But the king of fear had blinded them to who they were. And now he hoped to make that blindness permanent. But Yeshua had another plan. One that involved a young boy named Jack.

The dragon king's voice rumbled through the Valley of Death. "You have drunk from my queens' milk and received scales to protect you. Today you will drink from me, and I will turn those scales black to seal our union forever!"

The dragon king wanted them to drink from him as Jack had done, blinding them even more. His heart pounded. What if the Scalers were beyond reach after they drank from the dragon king? It had nearly destroyed him. Yes, he had found a way, but would they?

His chest began to burn, and at first he thought it was only the pain he was feeling for the Scalers. But then an image of Zevonus flashed through his mind.

The silver ring. It still rested on his skin under his clothes. Zevonus had said he would know what to do with it when the time came. Surely, the time had come. He still didn't know what to do, but he was sure that if he just stepped forward in faith, Yeshua's light would guide him.

Jack pushed himself to his feet, and the dragon king turned dark eyes to him, taken aback.

Help me, Yeshua. Show me your light and guide my mind.

Jack took a step into the abyss of uncertainty, as if he were stepping out of a boat into an ocean that would surely swallow him. All he had now was faith in Yeshua. And like Yeshua, he would have to walk on water.

He could feel the eyes of the other Scalers on his back. He could feel their fear intensify—fear not only for him, but for themselves.

The dragon king parted his jaws to speak, but Jack spoke before he could, taking another step.

"Yea, though I walk through the valley of the shadow

of death, I will fear no evil," he said, reciting a prayer his mother had taught him. Another step forward. Stillness gripped the canyon. The king stood frozen, caught off guard.

"Because I do not walk alone," Jack continued, raising his voice so that it echoed off the cliffs for everyone to hear. "I stand in the light and love of Yeshua."

The Reds' shrieks of torment started in the back, far behind Jack, and swept forward as they betrayed their own fear of his words. The king's dark eyes cut to slits and he growled, dripping fangs exposed.

Another step forward. Jack reached for the ring inside his shirt.

"A love that casts out all fear," he cried. "A light that dispels the darkness!"

The ring was in his hand and he could feel its heat running up his arm. He didn't have to look to know his scales were falling off.

The Scalers gasped as the black scales plopped to the ground like coins falling out of a purse. The Reds' cries of rage grew, echoing all around him, and the king was speaking to his mind, words filled with hatred and terrible threats. Jack ignored them. They were just lies.

He took another step. "Because even in the Valley of Death, death is but a shadow."

The king let out a thunderous roar, and a thousand

Reds lifted into the air as one. Jack kept his eyes on the king, who was a lie, his darkness only a shadow that would be gone in the light. He'd never been more certain of anything.

The Reds came then, diving from the sky directly toward Jack, shrieking. A familiar voice was crying out to him—Sammie, screaming for him to run.

For a moment, Jack wondered if he'd made a mistake. Maybe his place was to die here, shredded by talons of a hundred dragons. But the doubt left quickly. He knew what he should do.

He slipped the ring onto his ring finger, balled his hand into a fist, and thrust it into the air. A forcefield of light erupted from the ring, like a shield made of truth.

The leading Reds were coming too quickly to stop their momentum, and they slammed into the light like birds flying into glass. Their large red-scaled bodies bounced off the protective barrier and fell to the ground in heaps, motionless.

Still they came in a hopeless determination to break through the light. In wave after wave, the red dragons tumbled to the ground and laid where they fell.

Jack leapt up on the stone platform, ignoring the queens, who bellowed in fury, wings spread and lips pulled back to reveal teeth sharp enough to rip a tree in two. But they weren't attacking. They were backing away, leaving him for their king, who was silenced by the carnage of his minions.

Thunder crashed overhead and Jack saw massive black clouds rolling in, darkening the sky and sending jagged bolts of white-hot current to the earth. Wind tore at his hair and clothes. The prince of the air who ruled this world in fear was in the full throes of rage.

Lightning struck the platform, igniting a fire. Flames leapt to the air in a full circle that surrounded Jack and the king, separating them from the rest of the hive. The heat threatened to melt Jack's skin, but he held firm, facing the world's fear.

The king filled his chest and released a long, thundering roar. Toxin-laced breath struck Jack full in the face, filling his nostrils, stinging his eyes, threatening to knock him off his feet.

Jack had never felt the depth of terror that tore through him as the toxin swallowed him. Dark enough to blot out the sun, heavy enough to flatten a forest. Jack braced himself, leaning forward.

"You have no power but the power I give you by agreeing to fear!" Jack screamed. "But I am one with Yeshua in light and love!"

The dragon king glared at him, momentarily stunned by that single truth. But then his face twisted in rage.

"Fool!" he snarled. "You cannot be free of me! I have always ruled this world!"

Jack mustered all the courage he had and managed a step froward. Then another. He knew now what he must do, but to do it, he had to be closer.

"I own this world!" the dragon king roared. "It has been bound to me in the hearts of all from the beginning! Even those who claim love breathe of me!"

Jack pushed forward through the fear battering his mind and soul.

"I am fear! I am this world! Nothing can . . ."

Jack sprinted then, while the dragon king was lost in his own praise. Ringed hand snatching free the silver knife at his waist, feet faster than humanly possible, Yeshua's power flowing through his bones. His voice certain, screaming into the sky.

"I am in this world, but no longer of it! I am the boy from the stars, and in Yeshua's love I am the love that casts out fear!"

Jack threw his feet forward and slid on his back toward the beast's underbelly. Before the king could react, he thrust the dagger upward and sliced the monster's underbelly from chest to tail.

Light exploded from the ring, ripped up through the dagger, and filled the dragon king.

Then Jack was past the black-scaled beast, coming to his feet in one smooth motion just before the wall of fire.

Jack spun around, dagger in hand, black blood dripping from its glowing blade. The king had gone perfectly still as the light of love raged through him. Yeshua's words flashed through Jack's mind. His kingdom was taken by great force—the light of love that ended all fear.

The king lifted his head and uttered a bellowing groan, surely knowing his end had come. And it had. Because in the next moment, the light erupted from his bowels, obliterating all that was once dragon. A huge ball of blinding light engulfed the stone platform, snuffed out the ring of fire, and then was gone, leaving only Jack and a tendril of smoke where the king had stood.

Then even that smoke vanished.

The king was no more. The light of love had so easily overcome fear.

Jack looked down at the glowing dagger in his hand and the silver ring that had turned it to light. Drawn by a deep knowing, Jack walked to the center of the blazing circle of fire, dropped to one knee, and plunged the white-hot dagger into the stone platform.

Light exploded from the platform, blasting out in every direction. As it crossed over the Valley of Death, it brought new life, leaving a meadow of bright green grass and beautiful white flowers in its wake.

Still on one knee, Jack looked around, stunned by the transformation of the land. The queens were gone. As were the Reds, leaving the cliffs empty. They couldn't exist without the dragon king.

The Scalers stood on the grass fifty paces from him, gawking at the change. Like the Valley of Death itself, their bodies were free of the effects of the dragons' curse—scales gone and eyes clear. But even so, Jack knew fear was still in their minds. As Yeshua had said, the dragons lived in the minds of all, and each would choose to serve it or to serve love.

He would share Yeshua's love with them, but the choice would be theirs.

Jack left the dagger embedded in the stone. He stood, legs shaky. He took a deep breath and exhaled slowly. He had done it. He'd slayed the dragon of fear that manifested on Earth following the great religious wars, which themselves were staggering expressions of fear.

A soft tweet sounded to his right, and Jack watched a flock of white doves fly through the valley, twirling in the air in a show of acrobatic excellence. The sound of heavy wings flapping drew his gaze up, and what he saw filled him with wonder. A large silver dragon was gracefully descending.

Zevonus!

Others also came, flying in low over the stone cliffs. He couldn't believe what he was seeing. As if they had never been slaughtered, the Silvers arrived unmarked and whole. They swooped down and landed on the right side of the platform.

A young, vivacious dragon pushed through the others, blue eyes bright and eager.

"Zeke!" Jack shouted, leaping from the platform. He rushed up and threw his arms around the young Silver's leg. "You're alive!"

"Young Jack!" Zeke said, speaking in his mind. The Silver lowered his head and nuzzled Jack's cheek. For a moment, Jack thought his heart might explode.

"I thought you were dead," Jack croaked.

"You think Yeshua's spirit can die?" Zeke asked with a wink. Then he raised his head and looked past Jack. "He works in mysterious ways."

A small fearful cry from a child filled Jack's ears. He turned to see what Zeke was seeing. The Scalers, still gripped by fear, were staring at the Silvers.

Jack walked toward them. The Village Mother stepped in front of the others, her arm reaching back to hold them in place like a mother trying to protect her children. Jack slowed. They still didn't understand what had happened here.

The Village Mother's eyes brimmed with tears. "What have you done to us?" Her voice was thin. "You killed the dragons!"

"Yes," Jack said. "You don't have to be afraid anymore."

The Village Mother looked about, disoriented. "They kept us safe. And you've brought back our enemy? You've ruined us!"

Jack wasn't surprised by her reaction. The Scalers had spent so long living with the Reds that they probably couldn't imagine living without them. It would take time for them to see there was another way, the way of Yeshua's love, which can not be disturbed by anything. Not even red dragons.

Jack heard heavy steps behind him and twisted to see Zevonus approaching. The large Silver stopped twenty feet from them, eyes on the Scalers. In response, Lukas stepped out from the Scalers and walked toward the massive Silver. The greatest dragon hunter the Scalers had ever known now had his clear eyes locked with the oldest Silver who had ever lived.

Lukas stopped fifteen feet from Zevonus. "Forgive me," he said.

"All is forgiven in love," Jack heard Zevonus say.

The young man raised his head with tears on his cheeks. "How are any of you alive?" He turned to Jack. "And how could a boy destroy the dragon king?"

"Because the dragon king, like all Reds and their queens, was only fear. And fear is a lie," Jack said. "The Silvers are the spirit of love, which cannot die. I could kill the king because I surrendered to Yeshua's love, which casts out all fear."

Lukas stared for a moment. "You've said this before, but I didn't understand." He hesitated. "You've told me about this Yeshua, but I wasn't listening. Will you tell me again?"

Jack nodded. Then he turned back to the other Scalers. "I will tell anyone who wants to hear."

CHAPTER SIXTEEN

IT TOOK some convincing to persuade the Scalers to fly back to their village on the backs of Silvers, but the only other route was a two-week walk over towering mountains, a prospect that terrified them even more. Many feared other Reds would find them and tear them limb from limb. Lukas finally convinced his mother, pointing out that the Silvers could have killed him. They could have taken revenge on all the Scalers. Instead, they had forgiven.

Upon returning to their home, they discovered that the dragon's skull mounted at the village center as well as all the dragon milk had vanished. Only the altar remained.

That night, many gathered around the large firepit where they'd celebrated fear and listened to Jack talk about Yeshua's love. Lukas had been the first to accept the way of love.

"I will follow this way!" he boldly proclaimed, standing tall.

Zevonus brought healing water from a fountain in the Silver Temple, and Jack offered it to Lukas as a symbol of the living water Yeshua offered. He'd drained the ladle and tossed it back to Jack. "Truth be told, I always hated dragon milk anyway," he said with a smirk. Some chuckled. Others weren't eager to dismiss the lie they'd believed for so long.

But by the following morning, all followed Lukas in rejecting the Reds and embracing Yeshua's love. Jack was certain the small jar containing Zevonus's gift of water would run out of water, but it seemed to be bottomless, like the love of Yeshua himself. Jack had never felt so full of life. He could hardly stand still as Scaler after Scaler became lovers of the light, even Camila and the Village Mother, who were among the last. How could they not drink the Silver's water after seeing love's crushing power over the king of fear?

Overjoyed, the Scalers destroyed all reminders of their old way. They tore down the metal poles that once held up the skull of terror and comfort. They broke down the altar. They cried and laughed and spoke of new beginnings.

Fear was still there, in their minds, Jack knew. For that to be gone, each would follow Yeshua's journey of transformation. Failing to follow that path had been religion's great challenge in the last age. He would point them to Yeshua's way.

"Are there other Scalers on Earth somewhere?" Jack asked Zevonus before he left with the other Silvers.

"Perhaps," Zevonus answered. "But not in these mountains." He didn't elaborate.

"What about Reds?" Jack pushed.

"Again, not in these mountains. But they live in the minds of most. Fear will always try to blind you to love, young Jack. We Silvers will never be far from you. The awakening to Yeshua's love is not yet finished."

Jack understood. One day, they would need to go beyond these mountains and offer Yeshua's love to everyone they found.

Jack wasn't sure how often or even if he'd see the Silvers again, but he knew he would keep them close to his heart forever. The whole village gathered as the great dragons bid them farewell and took to the skies. It was a magnificent sight.

But something else hovered in Jack's mind.

His mother.

The events of recent days had been so consuming—first in great fear following the king's mission, then in great triumph as love restored them all—that Jack hadn't fixated on his mother. But as the Silvers disappeared over the horizon, worry nipped at his mind.

He'd sent the village's coordinates to the Sanctuary at the king's orders, but they hadn't arrived. Were they still coming? Had they run out of oxygen? Was his mother still alive?

A part of him wanted to rush back to the shuttle to send another message. He would if they didn't arrive soon.

As it turned out, he didn't need to, because the village filled with a roar at dusk, drawing every soul out to point at a huge ship coming from the sky. They all watched the Arc make its final descent into the field on the village outskirts.

Within minutes the door hissed open. The first to emerge was his mother, followed by the rest—all of them staring around at the villagers in confusion. There was much to explain, but for now all Jack cared about was his mother.

He rushed forward and threw his arms around her. "Mom!"

She began to weep, wrapping him in an embrace. "Oh, Jack! I knew it! I just knew it!" She took his face in her hands and looked him over. "Are you hurt? Is everything okay?"

He grinned up at her. "More than okay, Mom." Then he grabbed her hand and tugged her away from them all. "Come."

She came, stumbling after him. He spun back and yelled at Sammie, who was scanning the new arrivals for her mother. "Tell them everything, Sammie! We'll be back."

Then he led her to the hill south of the village and sat her on a large boulder. There, pacing before her like the boy he was, he began to tell her everything that had happened, beginning with their crash-landing.

She let him talk, asking him for clarifications as he stumbled through the whole story, often retracing his steps and offering more detail. He was just too excited to get it all straight in one telling.

They returned to the village when the sun set, and there he explained more, introducing her to Lukas and Camila and the Village Mother. After the evening celebration of Yeshua's love, he led her to one of the tree houses that had once been a lookout for silver dragons.

They spent that night lying under the stars, talking until he finally drifted off. This time he told her about seeing Yeshua. He couldn't say for sure if the encounter had been Yeshua in the flesh, but it was in his heart and mind. He doubted the man was actually walking around Earth, but his mother didn't care. It was the same either way, she said. And she couldn't have been more delighted.

Three days later, Jack walked through the bustling village looking at the faces of people he knew, some from Earth and others from space. They numbered nearly four hundred now. Before the Arc's arrival, Jack had warned the villagers that those who lived in space might not be eager to consider the love of Yeshua, because they hadn't seen the difference between fear and love as clearly as the villagers had. It would take time.

Regardless, both populations had been rescued from terrible trouble, and the glow of being alive brightened the eyes of all.

He acknowledged each person as he made his way through the village. He still wore the silver ring Zevonus had given him. It was a symbol of love's great power for the villagers, who'd seen that love defeat the dragon king. They all knew that Jack hadn't freed them from the Reds—Yeshua's love had done that. But Jack had been willing to follow the path of love, and the villagers placed some significance in that. Jack didn't, but the ring was a dear reminder of the Silvers, who would never leave them.

The captain, who they now called Robert, was deep in discussion with several carpenters, likely working through plans to build enough houses for four hundred souls. No one wanted to sleep inside the cave. Robert would help oversee the task of rebuilding before winter came.

Lieutenant Rover, who asked to be called Lieutenant, showed his frustration with a pully system Lukas was trying to explain. He was having a hard time adjusting to the primitive technology. Jack chuckled.

The older boy had truly become Jack's brother. He had a ravenous appetite for knowledge about Yeshua, and Jack had spent hours sitting with him through recent days, sharing. Jack's mother had suggested they read the ancient texts together, an idea that thrilled Lukas.

Camila and Sammie walked into the village from the eastern woods, a deer they'd just harvested slung over Camila's shoulders. Sammie said something to Camila and then hurried to Jack. He was thrilled to have his best friend back.

"Good hunting?" Jack asked.

"Camila's a good teacher," Sammie said.

"It helps that you're excellent with a bow," he pointed out.

"There is that," she said, then glanced across the village at Lukas and the lieutenant. "Lukas is still trying to teach Rover how their pully system works? I bet Camila Lieutenant won't rest until he's in charge."

Jack chuckled. "I'm pretty sure he wishes he was still in space."

Silence filled the space between them for a moment. "It's crazy when you think about all that's happened since we were up there."

"Yeah, everything is different," Jack said.

Sammie looked at him. "You're not that different," Sammie said. "Maybe that's why it had to be you in the end."

"How so?"

"A good leader needs to see everyone in equal light, not favoring some over others. That's you."

He smiled. "Maybe. I really thought I was going to lose you, Sammie."

She huffed and playfully pushed Jack's arm. "Yeah right. Like you could get rid of me that easily." She glanced away. "Not even an evil dragon king could separate us for long."

Jack loved Sammie in a way he wasn't sure he understood himself. Not yet anyway.

"Oh good," a familiar voice said behind Jack. "I need a hand."

Jack turned and saw his mother carrying a large basket of berries. Sammie and Jack hurried to her side and Sammie grabbed the basket.

"I got this." To Jack, "See you later?"

"Of course."

Then she was off.

"I have more," his mother said.

"More?"

"Well, lots of mouths to feed, and I found a patch of wild strawberries." She motioned to a burlap sack that hung on a branch. "Grab that bag and follow me." She turned and headed back into the trees.

Jack glanced at the large white Arc south of the village. It jutted up into the sky, a reminder of where they had come from. It was good to be back on Earth breathing fresh air and harvesting strawberries, just as he and his mom had always dreamed of doing.

He plucked a bag from the tree and caught up with her. "Wild strawberries?" Jack asked.

"As wild as they come. The soil here is amazing. We'll be able to grow plenty of food for everyone."

His mother slowed and looked down at him, a twinkle in her eye. "Can you see it still?"

She was talking about God, who was everywhere at once. God, who was one with Yeshua. And so was Jack now.

He closed his eyes and looked at the forest through the eyes of Yeshua. Light shined from everything in his field of view. He didn't know how long he'd be able to see this way, but he prayed it would never change.

A smile pulled at the corner of his mouth and his mother giggled.

"You could see it too if you wanted," Jack said. Something he'd told her a dozen times.

"I know, but I have more judgment than you. I'm working on it." She placed her arm around his shoulders as they walked on.

"Tell me again—all the things Yeshua said to you," she said.

"They're mostly the things you taught me," Jack said. "He was reminding me of what I already knew, because of you. I just hadn't experienced it myself. Few really have."

She smiled and he saw a tear slip down her cheek. "Your father would be so proud of you."

Emotion caught in Jack's throat as they walked

through the forest. "Sometimes I wonder what he would have thought about dragons."

His mother laughed and shook her head. "He would have loved the idea of dragons! Well, at least the Silvers."

"You know, if you ever want to meet one," Jack said, "maybe they'd come. Zeke could take us for a ride."

"Ride a dragon?" His mother laughed nervously and shook her head. "I think I'll stick with growing plants."

A great warmth spread through Jack's chest. This was the only moment that mattered. Here in the forest with his mother, the air clean, the planet full of life. The past was gone and the future would come.

For now, he'd just walk with his mother, see the light in all things, and talk about plants.

The End

WANT MORE?

Read the second dragon trilogy,
The Dragons Among Us,
the thrilling tale of Jack's son,
Noah, and his amazing journey
into the world of dragons.

MORE
ADVENTURE AWAITS

Discover the entire
Dekker young reader universe at

WWW.TEDDEKKER.COM